## "I didn't [hire you] to be my mistress,"

he said succinctly. "I don't intend to."

Pursing her lips, she said tautly, "I sincerely hope not, Mr. Donovan. Just because I didn't file a complaint against my boss at Liddell, doesn't mean I'll go along with anything as cheap as—"

He caught her by the wrist. "Ten grand isn't cheap," he said quickly. His nostrils flared and his eyes sparked. "And don't get the wrong impression about me. If I wanted to sleep with you, I wouldn't go about it this way."

She wanted to slap him, but the fingers curling over her wrist were clenched so tight she barely dared breathe. There was a power running through him as charged as an electric current, leashed by the thin hold he was keeping on his patience. And yet, she couldn't help but bait him. "No?" she goaded, tilting her head back. "And just how would you go about seducing me?"

"You want a demonstration?"

Dear Reader,

Happy Spring! April 1990 is in full bloom—the crocuses are bursting forth, the trees are beginning to bud and though we have an occasional inclement wind, as Shelley wrote in *Ode to the West Wind*, "O Wind, If Winter comes, can Spring be far behind?"

And in this special month of nature's rebirth, we have some wonderful treats in store for you. Silhouette Romance's DIAMOND JUBILEE is in full swing, and this month discover *Harvey's Missing* by Peggy Webb, a delightful romp about a man, a woman and a lovable dog named Harvey (aka George). Then, in May, love is in the air for heroine Lara MacEuan and her handsome, enigmatic hero, Miles Crane, in *Second Time Lucky* by Victoria Glenn.

The DIAMOND JUBILEE—Silhouette Romance's tenth anniversary celebration—is our way of saying thanks to you, our readers. To symbolize the timelessness of love, as well as the modern gift of the tenth anniversary, we're presenting readers with a DIAMOND JUBILEE Silhouette Romance title each month, penned by one of your favorite Silhouette Romance authors. In the coming months, writers such as Marie Ferrarella, Lucy Gordon, Dixie Browning, Phyllis Halldorson—to name just a few—are writing DIAMOND JUBILEE titles especially for you.

And that's not all! Pepper Adams has written a wonderful trilogy—*Cimarron Stories*—set on the plains of Oklahoma. And Laurie Paige has a heartwarming duo coming up— *Homeward Bound*. Be sure to look for them in late spring/ early summer. Much-loved Diana Palmer also has some special treats in store during the months ahead....

I hope you'll enjoy this book and all of the stories to come. Come home to romance—Silhouette Romance—for always!

Sincerely,

Tara Hughes Gavin
Senior Editor

# LISA JACKSON

# His Bride
# to Be

*Silhouette* **Romance**

Published by Silhouette Books New York

**America's Publisher of Contemporary Romance**

SILHOUETTE BOOKS
300 E. 42nd St., New York, N.Y. 10017

ISBN: 0-373-08717-9

First Silhouette Books printing April 1990

Printed in the U.S.A.

**Books by Lisa Jackson**

# *LISA JACKSON*

was raised in Molalla, Oregon, and now lives with her husband, Mark, and her two sons in a suburb of Portland, Oregon. Lisa and her sister, Natalie Bishop, who is also a Silhouette author, live within earshot of each other. The two sisters feel lucky to be doing what they love to do best—writing romances.

# *Chapter One*

Damn it, Leigh, I was counting on you!'' Hale Donovan swore loudly, not caring that the door to his office was ajar and his secretary could hear his every word. He stretched the telephone cord tight, pacing across thick fawn-colored carpet and wishing he could ring Leigh Carmichael's beautiful neck. As he glared out the window of his office, twenty stories above the crowded streets of San Francisco, he clenched his fingers tightly around the receiver. Outside, the lofty spires of the city's skyscrapers rose against the vibrant California-blue sky.

Hale barely noticed—he was too furious.

All he could see was the entire deal with Stowell Investments going down the proverbial drain. He'd been a fool to trust Leigh; she was cut from the same cold cloth as his mother, Jenna Donovan, a woman he could barely remember.

"Hale, you still there, darling?" Leigh's husky voice sounded over the wires, and she chuckled softly.

"Of course I'm still here," he snapped back.

"Good. Then you understand."

"What I understand is that you're reneging. Why?" he asked, knowing Leigh was trying to manipulate him. Again.

"I'm not interested in pretending," she said sulkily.

He could almost hear the wheels turning in her mind half a world away.

"I can't see ruining my vacation in Marseilles just to save your neck."

"You picked one helluva time to tell me! The cruise starts Friday!"

"Well, then, if you want me to go so badly, maybe you should make the engagement official," she suggested, her voice sultry and suggestive.

"What're you trying to do, Leigh? You know the whole thing's an act."

"Not to me. The only way I'll come back to San Francisco and pose as your fiancée is if you really want me to be your wife!"

Shoving one hand through his hair in frustration, Hale dropped to the corner of his desk. His eyes narrowed thoughtfully as he conjured up her face—a gorgeous face—with high cheekbones, pouty lips and ice-cold jade-green eyes. "Just what is it you want, Leigh? A ring?"

"Not just any ring, Hale. A diamond ring with at least three sparkling carats, and a promise that we'll walk down the aisle within the next two months."

He laughed. She was joking. She had to be! Their affair had ended six months before and they were both happier without the entanglements of a relationship. He yanked off his tie and slung it over the back of his chair. "Look, Leigh, I don't have time for games."

"This isn't a game."

For the first time he heard the undercurrents in her voice—the thread of steel running through her words. "I don't want marriage, Leigh. I'm not cut out for it. Neither are you."

"That's where you're wrong," she wheedled. "I think I'd be perfectly content to become Mrs. Hale Donovan."

"Damn it, Leigh—"

"Call me back if you change your mind."

The receiver on her end of the line clicked loudly in his ear.

Muttering, Hale slammed the receiver back into its cradle. In a way he was relieved. Two weeks of pretending to be in love with Leigh would have been hell. However, he needed a woman to pose as his wife-to-be before he set sail on William Stowell's yacht on Friday. Only a fiancée would prevent Stowell's daughter, Regina, from throwing herself at him.

Frowning, he strode to the bar and splashed brandy into a short crystal glass. He wanted to buy out William Stowell so badly he could taste it, but he wasn't willing to marry William's daughter, Regina, just to clinch the deal. Unfortunately she was scheduled on the cruise, as well.

Twenty years old, spoiled and sullen, Regina had continually pursued Hale for the past six months. Hale wasn't interested. Not in Regina, and especially not in marriage.

As far as he was concerned, marriage was a trap. What he needed was a woman—a woman he didn't know—a woman who would agree to pose as his intended for two weeks, then conveniently drop out of sight once he'd bought out William Stowell's shares of Stowell Investment Company. Hale's lips compressed into a cold grimace as he sipped his brandy. He would call Paul

Hastings in Personnel and tell Paul to find him a woman who had beauty, brains, charm and, most important of all, a vast, unsatiated greed!

Valerie Pryce shifted uneasily in her chair and waited. Across an expansive mahogany desk, the personnel director of Donovan Enterprises studied her résumé as if it were the Emancipation Proclamation.

A short man with a neatly cropped red beard, stiff white shirt and expensive pin-striped suit, Paul Hastings fingered his collar. "You graduated from UCLA in business two years ago."

"That's right." Valerie managed a smile that felt forced. She couldn't let Hastings know how much she needed a job—any job.

"And while you went to school you supported yourself by modeling and acting?"

"Just a few commercials and a small role on a soap opera." What did that have to do with anything? she wondered. Smoothing her skirt and hoping she didn't look as nervous as she felt, she met his gaze evenly.

"But you didn't want an acting career?"

"The jobs dried up."

"Oh." He scanned the first page. "You're single."

Valerie bristled a little, but reminded herself that she needed this job. "Yes."

"Never been married?"

"No."

"What about boyfriends?"

"I don't think that's any of your business," she said, clamping her hands over the arms of her chair.

He lifted a palm. "You're right, of course. Just asking." Paul tilted his chair back and stared at her, his eyes narrowing behind thick glasses as he took in her features. "I'd like you to meet Hale Donovan."

"The president of the company?" she repeated, stunned. Good Lord, why?

Stuffing her résumé into a file, Paul chuckled. "Around here we refer to him as God . . . or Lucifer. Depending on his mood."

"Sounds charming," Valerie observed.

"He can be." Paul dialed the phone, spoke quickly into the receiver, then shoved back his chair and led Valerie through a maze of hallways to a private elevator. He punched out the number for the twentieth floor, and the doors slid shut.

"Is it normal for anyone applying for a job as an administrative assistant to meet Mr. Donovan?" she asked as the elevator groaned and started to climb.

"It is when they're applying to become Mr. Donovan's personal assistant."

Valerie nearly gasped. Personal assistant to Hale Donovan? "That's the job?"

Paul slanted her a nervous glance. "It just opened up yesterday afternoon. Ah, here we are." He waited for her to exit, waved at a tiny gray-haired receptionist behind a spacious desk and smiled. "He's expecting us, Madge."

Without missing a beat at her word processor, Madge nodded and Paul shoved open one of two gleaming cherry-wood doors.

Valerie drew in a deep breath. Since she'd first set foot inside Donovan Enterprises less than an hour before, she'd been shuffled from one office to another, spoken with several assistants in personnel and finally landed here, in front of Hale Donovan's office, reading his name engraved in brass as she was bustled inside. She braced herself. She hadn't expected an interview with God himself.

Hale heard the door open and wished Paul Hastings would just go away. Since the previous afternoon, when he'd called and demanded to meet a woman to pose as his bride-to-be, he'd interviewed nearly forty would-be Mrs. Hale Donovans. Forty of the most self-centered, vain and nervous women he'd ever seen. None had come even close. He couldn't imagine spending two hours cooped up with any of them, and the thought of two weeks aboard a yacht as he pretended to care about one of those shallow, self-directed women turned his stomach.

He was beginning to think his plan wasn't worth the effort.

Paul cleared his throat.

Rubbing the back of his neck, Hale turned, disinterested until his gaze collided with the serious eyes of a tall, slender woman who held herself with a bearing that could only be described as regal. Her hair was honey blond, highlighted with pale streaks and swept away from her face in a French braid. Wearing a magenta blouse and black skirt that matched her oversized jacket, she crossed the room.

Large, intelligent hazel eyes rimmed in curling dark lashes peered at him, and the tilt of her chin was bold, nearly defiant. Her cheekbones were high, tinged pink, and her lips were curved into a wary smile. "Funny," she said, staring boldly at Hale, "I never pictured God wearing blue jeans."

Paul inhaled swiftly and looked as if he'd just swallowed something much too large for his throat. Choking, he shot the woman a warning glance and made hasty introductions. "Hale Donovan, this is—"

"Valerie Pryce," she said, extending her hand.

Hale clasped her slim fingers, and was surprised at the strength in her grip.

"Ms. Price brought her résumé in this afternoon. She's looking for a job with the company."

"She's not from an agency?" Hale was surprised—he'd pegged Valerie for a model, a sophisticated New York type.

Paul shook his head. "No, she's a walk-in, but I think she'll work out," he said, eyeing Valerie curiously. "Her résumé's in here." He placed the file folder on the corner of Hale's desk. "Keep me posted."

"I will."

Paul exited, closing the door behind him.

"I think you made him nervous," Hale said, amusement flickering in his gaze.

"I didn't mean to."

Hale twisted his thin lips. "He's had a long day."

"So I gathered." She watched this man cautiously. He simply wasn't a typical executive, at least not in her opinion. Dressed in faded jeans and a blue cambric shirt with its sleeves shoved over his forearms, he looked as though he belonged on a ranch, or in the back lot of a movie studio, working as a stuntman on a B-grade Western, not in a chrome-and-glass office decorated with metal objets d'art and tan leather.

His hair needed to be trimmed; black locks curled over his collar and his jaw was dark with a day's growth of beard. His features, all angles and blades, fitted into a face that was too rugged to be called Hollywood handsome. A long nose separated hollow cheeks and stopped just short of a thin, almost cruel mouth. His looks might have been classified as severe, had it not been for his eyes. Steel gray and deep set, guarded by thick black brows and long straight lashes, they were lit by an inner spark, a flicker of humor.

He picked up her résumé, scanning it as he crossed an expanse of thick carpet to an overstuffed leather chair.

She noticed how easily his legs and buttocks moved beneath the denim—fluidly, gracefully, though she sensed a restlessness to him. He seemed to have the coiled energy of a caged animal.

"You worked for Liddell International?"

"Two years."

He nodded thoughtfully. "Why'd you quit?"

"It was time," she said.

"It *is* my business, you know."

"Only if you hire me."

Sighing, he dropped onto the arm of the contemporary chair. His gaze never left hers. "What happened? Liddell is a great company."

There was no reason to lie. He'd find out soon enough. "My boss and I had a . . . disagreement."

"About?"

Her lips twisted cynically. "Personal rights."

"Meaning?"

"Meaning he came on to me, okay?" she shot back angrily. "We were working late, he made a pass, I didn't respond and my career at Liddell died." There was more to it, of course. But she didn't think the fact that Brian Liddell, Jr. had expected her to sleep with him was any of Donovan's business.

Hale was staring at her. "That's sexual harassment," he said softly.

"I know."

"You could sue."

Drawing in a deep breath, she whispered, "I decided I'd just rather forget it. Besides, I don't have time for a law suit. I need to make a living."

Hale tried to ignore the compassion that moved him. He hadn't misinterpreted the flicker of pain in her eyes. Whatever had happened at Liddell had been more than just a simple come-on. Her hands shook a little as she tucked them into the pockets of her jacket. "Would you like a drink?" Standing, he crossed to the bar.

"No, thanks."

"You're sure?"

"I think I'll wait until after the interview." She seemed to draw from an inner strength, and though she had paled, she was facing him squarely again, having regained her composure.

"Did Paul tell you about the job?" Hale asked, opening louvered doors to the bar. Crystal stemware and shiny bottles sparkled from the soft recessed lights hidden above the mirrored backdrop.

"He didn't get that far. In fact, he was a little vague about the particulars," she said, deciding to get to the point. "All he told me is that I'm interviewing to become your personal assistant."

Hale's brows quirked as he reached for an opened bottle of brandy and a glass. "That's one way of putting it."

"Give me another."

He didn't turn around, but his gray gaze caught hers in the reflection of the mirror. "What I'm looking for, Ms. Pryce, is a woman who will pose as my fiancée for the next two weeks."

"Your fiancée?" she repeated.

He saw her catch her breath. A shadow of disappointment clouded her eyes, and she actually blushed.

"But I thought . . ."

"Paul should have been straight with you."

"It would have helped!" she snapped, her cheeks flaming. "What is this?"

"A simple business proposition," he replied, bemused at her outrage. At least he'd shocked her out of whatever secret was tormenting her.

"I don't like the sound of it."

"Just listen," he suggested, striding back to his desk and leaning a jean-clad hip against it. "I'm trying to buy out William Stowell of Stowell Investments. He and I are planning to hammer out a deal next week aboard his yacht. We'll be sailing up the coast to Canada. Unfortunately his daughter, Regina, is coming along, and William thinks I should marry her. Regina seems to agree." The corners of his mouth tightened. "I don't."

"So why don't you tell her so?"

Hale smiled faintly. "I have. More times than I want to count. She doesn't believe me. Neither does her father."

"You expect me to believe this?"

"It's true." Taking a long swallow of scotch, he studied her before placing the empty glass on his desk.

"It's crazy."

"A little," he agreed, shrugging. "But why would I make it up?"

*Good point!*

"Besides, it ensures me the company of a beautiful woman," he added, his eyes glinting.

"Does it?" She drew an outraged breath, slinging the strap of her purse over her shoulder with more aggression than necessary.

"The job is yours if you want it."

"No way."

"It could be interesting."

Was he serious? "What I need is a *real* job, Mr. Donovan. Not some insane scheme where I pose as your mistress. I didn't go to night school for three years to be paid to fawn all over you for two weeks. I think you'd better find someone else."

"There isn't time."

"Isn't time? Give me a break! I'm sure if you looked hard enough you could find any number of women who'd want to play house with you on a cruise. I just don't happen to be one of them."

"I'll make it worth your while."

"I guess you didn't hear me, Mr. Donovan. I'm not interested." She turned on her heel and marched through the double doors, sweeping past Madge in a cloud of indignation. How could she have been so stupid? Assistant to the president! Ha! The problem with anything that looks too good to be true is that it usually is!

Slamming her palm against the elevator call button, she fumed, waiting impatiently. From the corner of her eye she saw Hale Donovan, his jaw set as he strode toward her.

"Don't you want to hear me out?" he asked.

"No!"

"We haven't even talked about money."

"We don't need to."

A soft bell rang, and the elevator's doors parted. Gratefully Valerie stepped inside.

Hale followed, blocking the doors with his shoulder. "Give me five minutes. I'll bet I can convince you."

The nerve of the man! Narrowing her eyes, she hissed, "I don't have a price tag."

"Everyone does."

Ignoring him, she slapped the button for the first floor. The elevator didn't move.

"Think about it," he suggested.

"Oh, I will," she assured him, raising her chin a fraction, leveling her gaze at his arrogant face. "And I'll laugh."

Before he could stop himself, he reached forward, grabbing her arm quickly. The elevator lurched and the doors started to close before he stopped them with his foot. "I'll call you."

"Don't bother."

Madge appeared in the open door. Her anxious brown eyes flicked from Hale to Valerie and back again. "Paul's on the line. He wants to know how things worked out. There's another woman—"

"We don't need another woman," Hale said quietly, his eyes fixed on Valerie.

For a heart-stopping second, he clenched steely fingers over her arm.

"Tell Paul I've found the one I want."

## Chapter Two

Who was Valerie Pryce?

Hale stood at the glass wall behind his desk and watched the traffic and pedestrians swarming through Union Square.

The intercom buzzed, and Madge's raspy voice sounded. "Paul's on two."

"Got it." Hale picked up his receiver. "Donovan."

"I have a couple more women you might want to interview," Paul suggested, his voice sounding tired.

"Not interested."

"But—"

"Didn't Madge make it clear? I want Valerie Pryce." Hale paced from one end of his office to the other. The telephone cord stretched, then recoiled as he strode away from his desk, then back past it.

"Did you hire her?" Hastings asked, sounding mildly surprised.

"Not exactly." Hale waved impatiently. "She didn't sign a contract, but it's just a matter of time," he said, glancing nervously at his watch.

"Then she agreed?"

"Not in so many words—"

"I thought you wanted someone today."

"I do." Hale clenched his teeth. He knew he was being stubborn and unrealistic. The woman just plain didn't want the job. But he couldn't forget her. With the razor-edged intuition that had guided him over the years, he believed that Valerie Pryce was the woman who could pull this off. The challenge in her intriguing hazel eyes, her regal bearing and her quick, irreverent humor gave her the right combination of charm and class.

Paul brought him back to the conversation. "Well, if she's not working out, there are four women from the Jewell Woods Agency down here. Any one of them—"

"You're not listening, Paul," Hale cut in, picking up Valerie's résumé and scanning the two sheets of paper as if they held some clue to his fascination with her. "My fiancée for the next two weeks is going to be Valerie Pryce."

"You might tell her about it," Paul suggested, his voice tinged with more than a little sarcasm.

"I will. I'm on my way over there now."

"She might not agree."

"I'll convince her."

"How?"

"Come on, Hastings. Money talks." Hale reached for his leather jacket and swung it over one shoulder. "Call Kendrick in the legal department. Tell him what I want. A contract for two weeks—leave the amount of compensation blank. And give the name of personal assistant to the position."

"If I were you . . ."

Hale waited, listening, his fingers tight around the receiver. He heard Paul sigh in disgust.

"If I were you, I'd just be straight with William Stowell and forget all this phony engagement business."

"I tried that," Hale reminded him, his gut twisting as he remembered his last meeting with Stowell. William had hinted he'd like nothing better than to call Hale his son-in-law.

Obviously Regina had agreed. Behind her father's back, she'd come up with her own plan to trap Hale.

After six hours of heavy business negotiations and several drinks with Stowell, Hale had unlocked his hotel room door and found Regina, wrapped in nothing but pink silk sheets, lying across his bed. A bottle of champagne had been chilling in an ice bucket near the headboard. Regina had smiled coyly up at him, a dimpled come-hither grin pursing her lips, as he'd leaned heavily against the door frame.

"I've been waiting for you," she whispered in a clumsy attempt at seduction.

"How'd you get in?"

She smiled. "The desk clerk doesn't ask too many questions."

"I think you'd better leave," Hale muttered, angry she was there. He was tired, and all he wanted was a hot shower and a warm bed—a bed without Stowell's daughter.

"Not yet," she murmured.

"Now."

"We could have fun—"

"Your father would kill me, and I'd hate to think what he'd do to you."

"What Daddy doesn't know won't hurt him," she said, brows lifting as she sank her teeth into her lower lip.

"Forget it, Regina. I'm not interested."

"Why not?" she complained, holding the sheet around her and looking so young it had made his skin crawl.

"Look, it won't work," he said, and when he'd finally realized she wasn't about to budge, he'd left her, still wrapped in silk, her cheeks scorching red at his rejection.

Hale sighed in exasperation at the memory. Though he knew William wasn't behind Regina's advances, Hale didn't need a replay of that awkward scene. He also knew he couldn't spend the next two weeks with her—not unless he appeared to be off-limits.

On the other end of the line, Paul cleared his throat. "You're sure about this?"

"Positive. Send the models home and tell Kendrick to get everything in writing."

Valerie knocked once on the door of her mother's small apartment, then unlocked the dead bolt. "Mom?" she said softly as she entered. The shades were drawn, the air heavy and still.

Footsteps approached as Valerie closed the door behind her.

"She's resting," Belinda whispered, cocking her head toward the bedroom.

"Is she all right?"

"Better every day," Belinda said with a smile. A stocky woman with black hair pulled into a tight bun at the base of her skull, Belinda was a godsend. Since the accident in which her mother had been hit by a speeding car, Belinda, a private nurse who worked at a nearby hospital, had lived here, helping with Anna Pryce's care and recovery. "Your mother's a strong woman."

Valerie smiled. "She's had to be."

"I think she's awake."

"Good." Valerie walked down a short hall and shoved open the bedroom door.

Anna, thin and wan, was lying on her back, a sheet drawn to her chin. The only light in the room flickered from the television set. A hand-knit afghan was folded at the foot of the old double bed, and magazines and books littered every available surface of the bureau, night table and bookcase.

Valerie smothered a grin as she recognized the characters from her mother's favorite soap opera, *Life's Golden Sands*, the same daytime drama on which Valerie had once played a small role.

"So you're here, are you?" her mother murmured, struggling into a sitting position.

"I thought I'd stop by."

"How'd the interview go?"

Valerie tilted her hand in the air. "Not great. I think I'd better keep looking."

Anna, tucking a wayward lock of fine brown hair behind her ear, studied her daughter. "You had your heart set on Donovan Enterprises."

"There are other companies."

"But you've always said you liked the way Hale Donovan did business."

Valerie wrinkled her nose. "I've changed my mind. Besides, there wasn't a position open."

"But you saw it in the paper..." her mother protested, waving at a stack of newspapers near the bed.

"It had already been filled. But it doesn't matter. I've got callbacks at a couple other places."

"Well, if you ask me, whoever's in charge at Donovan Enterprises made a big mistake not hiring you!"

"I'll tell him the next time I see him," she replied with a grim smile. There were a lot of things she'd like to tell Mr. Donovan, but of course, she'd never get the chance. And that was probably a blessing, she reminded herself.

"Ask Belinda to make some coffee," her mother suggested. "And draw open the blinds—I swear, this place is like a tomb!"

Grinning, Valerie snapped open the shade. "I'll make the coffee. Belinda's got to get to the hospital."

Her mother skewered her with a knowing glance. "Then use the real coffee. I don't need any of that phony caffeine-free stuff."

"But your doctor—"

"Doesn't know a thing about coffee." Her mother grinned. "And don't waste any time. I think Lance is trying to kill Meredith!" her mother said, mentioning two long-running characters on *Life's Golden Sands*.

"He'll never get away with it," Valerie called over her shoulder as she started the coffee maker.

"Oh, what do you know?" her mother sang out, laughing quietly.

Belinda followed Valerie into the kitchen. "She's better today."

"I think so, too."

"But, then, I didn't show her these." Belinda reached into her purse and pulled out several small envelopes.

"Don't tell me—bills," Valerie guessed.

"Just six."

Valerie's stomach tightened. Not just six—six more.

Belinda chewed on her lower lip. "Look, I didn't want to tell you, but—"

Valerie waved her apology aside and managed a cheery smile. "Don't worry, I can handle it." She took the bills, stuffed them into her purse and waited as the coffee drizzled into a glass carafe.

"So how did the interview go?"

"Like gangbusters," Valerie muttered sarcastically as she poured two cups of hot coffee. "But I didn't get the job." She saw the lines knotting Belinda's smooth forehead and amended, "Well, actually, I could've taken one job, but it isn't the one I wanted." Thinking of Hale Donovan's outrageous proposal, she gritted her teeth. "Don't worry, there are lots of jobs. I'll find one this week."

"Sure you will." Belinda snagged her favorite navy-blue sweater from a hook near the door. "I'd better run. I'll see you tomorrow."

With a wave, Belinda left, and Valerie, carrying both steaming mugs to the back bedroom, ignored the little voice in the back of her mind that kept reminding her that she was running out of time and that, if she'd used her head, she should have at least heard Hale Donovan out.

"Forget it," she mumbled.

"Forget what?" her mother asked.

"Nothing. Now tell me—what's going on?" She handed her mother a cup and pretended interest in the program. "Lance won't kill Meredith," she predicted.

"Oh, and why not?"

"I just read that the actress has renegotiated her contract."

Her mother rolled her eyes. "You really know how to take the fun out of this, don't you?" But she chuckled and made a face as she took an experimental sip of coffee.

"Maybe Meredith will kill Lance," Valerie suggested.

"And she should, too," her mother agreed. "The way he's treated her..."

Two hours later Valerie climbed the triple flight of stairs to her apartment. She was still trying to push thoughts of Hale aside. Though she'd attempted to concentrate on anything but her interview with him, she could still hear his voice, see the image of his angular face, feel the mockery in his cold gray eyes. Fumbling with her key, she finally jammed it into the lock. "Bastard," she muttered.

She shoved the door open, and her gray tabby cat, Shamus, zipped out the door and onto the landing. "Miss me?" Valerie asked, bending down to pet his soft striped head. Purring loudly, he rubbed against her legs.

"I bet you're hungry, aren't you? Well, come on in, let's see what we've got."

Black-ringed tail aloft, Shamus trotted after her, then hopped onto a window ledge.

Valerie tossed her coat over the back of her daybed and kicked her shoes into the closet. Her apartment, which she fondly called the crow's nest, was little more than an attic loft tucked high in the gables of an old renovated row house in the Haight-Ashbury district. The ceilings sloped dramatically, the floors were polished oak, and aside from a walk-in closet, bathroom alcove and kitchen tucked behind folding doors, her entire living space consisted of this one room.

"And it's a great room," she told herself as she opened the folding doors to the kitchen, flipped on a burner and placed a kettle of water on the stove. She'd lived here since moving to San Francisco two years before and felt lucky to have an apartment with a view of the bay.

Pouring cat food into Shamus's dish, she called to him. "Well, come on." He hopped off the sill and landed not two feet from the bowl, sniffed disdainfully at the dry kiblets and cocked his head toward her as if he expected something more elegant.

"Sorry, boy, that's all we've got."

The kettle whistled shrilly. "My turn," she told the cat as she gave him one last pet, then scrounged in her cupboards for a tea bag of orange spice. She found one last bag, dunked it in the steaming water and soon the room was filled with the scents of oranges, cinnamon and cloves. Tomorrow, she thought, testing the tea, tomorrow she would look for another job. Not just any job, but a bona fide job that would pay enough to cover the bills and help support her mother. The kind of job she had hoped to find at Donovan Enterprises.

"Cross that one off the list," she murmured, conjuring Hale Donovan's image. His features swam before her eyes, and she frowned thoughtfully as she sipped the hot tea. Handsome? Yes. Arrogant? Definitely. Intriguing? No...well, yes.

She wished she'd never laid eyes on him. Yanking the pins from her hair, she leaned back, cradled the warm cup in her hands and sighed. Shamus leaped onto the couch and curled next to her.

With an effort, she closed her mind to Hale Donovan and concentrated on the next few days. She had to find a job and fast. Tomorrow she'd send out more copies of her résumé, call a couple of leads and— A loud rap on the door startled her, and Hale Donovan's voice boomed through the panels. "Valerie?"

Her heart did a peculiar flip, and she jumped, nearly spilling her tea. *Donovan? Here? Now?*

"Valerie? Are you in there?" He pounded loudly again.

Startled, Shamus flew off the couch and slunk behind a potted palm. "Chicken," Valerie muttered, though her own heart was hammering wildly.

"Valerie?" Hale called again.

"I'm coming, I'm coming," she said. She set her near-empty cup on a table, drew in a deep breath, then padded to the door in stocking feet. Peering through the peephole, she saw him, big as life, on the landing. Wearing a dark leather jacket and a grim expression, he leaned against the scarred mahogany railing. She'd hoped that his appearance had changed a little, that he wasn't as handsome as she'd recalled, but she'd been wrong. Hale Donovan in person was downright overwhelming. His arms were crossed over his chest, his eyes fastened on her door, his thin lips pursed impatiently.

"It's now or never," she whispered, steeling herself as she yanked open the door. Her stomach knotted as she stood squarely on the threshold. "What're you doing here?"

"I wasn't finished making you an offer."

"And I told you I wasn't interested."

"I know, I know, but I thought that by now you might have calmed down a little." He raked stiff fingers through his wavy, coal-black hair. "I didn't mean to offend you."

"No?" she mocked, wishing her insides would quit shaking and that she didn't find him so attractive and could simply listen to what he had to say.

"You didn't hear me out."

"Believe me, I heard enough."

His crooked smile caused her heart to trip.

"I suppose I did come on a little strong," he said.

"More than a little."

"Just give me a few minutes to explain," he suggested. "What've you got to lose?"

*Everything,* she thought wildly. This man distracted her far too much. His restless energy infected her. His glances cut deep, as if he were looking for something in her eyes—something elusive. Swallowing hard, she swung the door open and stepped aside. "You're wasting your breath."

"Mine to waste."

"Okay. Five minutes." Glancing pointedly at her watch, she closed the door behind him and stood, arms folded beneath her breasts, her back against the cool panels of the door, and waited.

Surveying the eclectic blend of art-deco paintings, antique tables and mismatched furniture, Hale said, "I want to offer you a job—a legitimate job." She started to protest, and he lifted a hand, silencing her. "Just hear me out. The title will be personal assistant, but, of course, you'll be more than that. You'll pretend to be my fiancée. Just for two weeks. Then the charade will be over. Think of it as an acting assignment."

"It's deception."

He nodded. "For a good cause."

"To thwart Regina Stowell's interest in you—I know. But she's your problem—not mine."

"And you could be the solution."

"I already told you I don't want the job. Deal with Regina Stowell yourself."

Jamming his fists into his pockets, he muttered, "Regina's twenty, spoiled and very stubborn."

"And you don't want to offend her father." She tossed her hair over her shoulder. "So you've cooked up this crazy scheme and expect me to run interference for you!"

"As I said, it's temporary."

"I'm still not interested."

Hale studied her. A captivating woman, Valerie Pryce. With wavy, uncombed blond hair framing a small, near-perfect face, her eyes shifting from gray to green, her brows puckered in frustration, she touched him in a way he hadn't been touched in a long, long while. It worried him a little, but not enough to convince him she wasn't the right woman. "I'm willing to pay ten thousand dollars."

Valerie sucked in a surprised breath. Her eyes widened, and she stared at him as if he truly had gone mad. "Ten thousand?" she repeated.

"Plus expenses."

She raised her chin a fraction, but he sensed she was wavering.

"I'm not for sale, Mr. Donovan."

"Think of it as rent."

Her eyebrows pulled together. "Rent? That's worse!"

But he could hear the hesitation in her voice, knew she was mulling over his offer. He felt a twinge of disappointment. So she did have a price, after all. "Look, you need a job, and I need you."

"Not me—any woman."

He shook his head. "A woman who will be believable as my fiancée. Neither Stowell nor his daughter would believe I'd just linked up with anyone."

"If you're trying to flatter me—"

"I am. And you should be. I've looked at women from every agency in town. None of them fit the bill. In order for someone to pose as my bride-to-be, she's got to be everything I'd want in a wife. She has to be more than beautiful, Valerie. She has to be smart, savvy and have a sense of humor."

"You don't know the first thing about me!"

A muscle worked in his jaw. "Ten thousand is a helluva lot of money for two weeks' work, which I should remind you is simply cruising up the Pacific coast on a private yacht, docking at Portland, Seattle, Victoria and anywhere else we want to! All you have to do is pretend to like me a little."

"That might be impossible," she shot back. What arrogance! "I think I'd have to put in three years at some Hollywood drama school before I could pull off an act like that."

He grinned—that irreverent slash of white that took her breath away.

"I'll make it easy on you," he said. "I'll try my best to be irresistible."

"You just don't know when to give up, do you?"

"I know what I want." He pierced her with his narrowed eyes.

Valerie swallowed against a suddenly dry throat. "And you think that whatever it is can be bought."

"Can't it?" he goaded.

Her temper, already strung tight, snapped. She crossed the small room in three swift strides and positioned herself squarely in front of Hale. "I came to Donovan Enterprises for a job, a real job! I can audit your books or program your computers. I've had experience working with attorneys as well as the IRS and I've even made coffee for the boss when I worked in the secretarial pool. But I've never, *never* been asked to pretend to be the boss's mistress!"

She was so close he could feel the heat radiating from her, see fire sparking in her eyes. "I didn't ask you to be my mistress," he said succinctly.

"Yet—"

"I don't intend to."

Pursing her lips, she said tautly, "I sincerely hope not, Mr. Donovan. Just because I didn't file a complaint against my boss at Liddell doesn't mean I'll go along with anything as cheap as—"

He caught her by the hand. "Ten grand isn't cheap," he said quickly, gripping her wrist. His nostrils flared, and his eyes sparked. "And don't get the wrong impression about me. If I wanted to sleep with you, I wouldn't go about it this way."

She wanted to slap him, but the fingers curling over her wrist clenched so tightly she barely dared to breathe. There was a power running through him as charged as an electric current, leashed by the thin hold he was keeping on his patience. And yet, she couldn't help bait him. "No?" she goaded, tilting her head back. "And just how would you go about seducing me?"

"You want a demonstration?" He slid his jaw to one side. His gaze, as fierce and bright as a silvery moon, delved into hers, then shifted pointedly to her mouth.

Valerie's breath lodged deep in her throat. Unconsciously she licked her lips. Hale stiffened, his gaze moving lazily from her lips to her eyes and back to the corner of her mouth.

She watched as his Adam's apple worked. For a breathless second she was sure he was going to kiss her. Her knees went weak at the thought that she'd pushed him too far. "I don't think a demonstration would be such a good idea," she whispered.

"Neither do I," he agreed, his mouth a thin line, his voice raw. Dropping her wrist, he stepped back a few paces, leaning his back against the wall and ramming his hands into the pockets of his jeans. "What I'm offering you, Ms. Pryce, is the chance to live the life of a princess for two weeks. And I'm willing to pay you very well for the opportunity. Most women—"

"I'm *not* like most women."

His head snapped up, and he impaled her with his sharp, magnetic gaze again. "I know. That's why I want you."

Her heart began to pound so crazily she thought he could surely hear it.

"Do we have a deal?"

If she had any pride at all, she thought, she would tell him to get out, to take his bloody offer and shove it. But she wasn't stupid, and unfortunately she needed the money. Ten thousand dollars would pay off her loan from college, help pay her mother's bills and leave enough of a nest egg to tide her over until she could find another job.

But what kind of strings were attached? She didn't know him, and couldn't let herself trust him. Why did she feel he was holding something back?

From the corner of her eye, she noticed Shamus sneaking toward the drapes. Valerie stalled. "Maybe I should talk this over with my roommate," she said.

"Your roommate?" He glanced around the room, and Valerie realized he was looking for any trace of a man.

Shamus ducked behind her rolltop desk. "Yes, uh, he and I discuss everything."

"He?" he repeated, turning back so his eyes could bore into hers. "But I thought—"

"Oh, it's nothing like that," she said hastily, enjoying her joke. "Very platonic..."

Hale glanced meaningfully down at the daybed. "Platonic." His jaw tightened, and at that moment Shamus poked his head from under the desk and sauntered over to Valerie, who reached down to pick him up.

"Meet Shamus," she said with a bright smile. "My roommate."

Hale wasn't amused. His eyes grew dark. Glancing pointedly at his watch, he muttered, "Our five minutes are over. So what's it going to be, Ms. Pryce?"

Valerie dropped the cat on the couch. She swallowed hard, trying to find her voice. "Okay," she finally agreed, trying to think rationally while her thoughts were spinning out of control. If she were going along with his crazy plan, she wanted some concessions—big concessions. "I'll do it. On...one—make that two—conditions."

"Name them."

"One—I don't sleep with you."

He twisted his lips into a lazy, disarming smile that caught her completely off guard.

"Agreed."

"Two—I want a contract that spells out the terms of my employment. And I want to work for you not just for two weeks, but for six months."

He clenched his jaw. "No way—"

"Oh, yes!" she insisted. "I want to prove to you that I can make it at Donovan Enterprises, and not just as a bimbo strutting around in a bikini, batting my eyelashes at you while we're sailing the seven seas!"

"Just one ocean," he corrected her.

"Look, Mr. Donovan—"

"Hale. We're engaged. Remember?"

" 'Hale,' " she repeated, "I've worked long and hard to get where I have. Just give me a chance. After the initial two weeks, I'll work for the same salary I was getting at Liddell."

"And how will we explain that we're no longer engaged?"

"Those things happen all the time."

"Not to me."

"This scheme was your idea," she reminded him. "It's got to be easier to break a phony betrothal than to pretend it exists."

"It would make more sense if we never saw each other again."

"Maybe so," she said, gambling. "But it's the only way I'll go along with it."

Hale hesitated as he reined in his temper. He shoved one hand through his hair in frustration. "You drive a hard bargain, Valerie."

"So do you."

Reaching into the pocket of his jacket, he withdrew an employment contract. "Got a pen?"

She found one in her purse and handed it to him.

Before he signed, he eyed her. "You are single, aren't you?" he asked.

"Very."

"Is there anything else that would prevent you from becoming my wife?"

She smiled at that. "You mean besides common sense? No."

"Good." Hesitating only a second, he pulled off the cap of the pen with his teeth, read the document, made a few quick slashes and scrawled an additional paragraph. After signing, he handed the contract to her.

She read it slowly, paragraph by straightforward paragraph. Hale had scratched in an additional clause, which lengthened the term of her employment from two weeks to six months and allowed her a salary of five hundred dollars more per month than she'd earned at Liddell. All in all, her employment with Donovan Enterprises was almost too good to be true.

Her stomach fluttered and her palms began to sweat.

"Satisfied?" he asked.

Nodding, she shoved aside all her nagging doubts, took the pen from his outstretched hand, then signed her name quickly on the line next to his. "There you go," she said, handing him back the single sheet. "When do I start?"

With a grin, he said, "Right now."

"Now—but I can't!"

Hale's eyes narrowed angrily. "We have less than forty-eight hours to get to know each other. I think we'd better get started."

"But—"

"Listen, Valerie," he said coldly. "You just signed on—the meter's running." He flopped onto the couch and leaned back as if he were incredibly weary. "Start at the beginning. Where you were born, if your parents are living and where. Tell me about your brothers and sisters—and if you've been married before."

The magnitude of what she'd just done hit her full force. There were a lot of things she'd rather keep secret from Hale Donovan—a private side of her she'd like to remain that way. "Just how much do you want to know about me?" she asked boldly, already regretting that she'd signed his damned contract.

"Everything."

She cleared her throat. "There are some things that are private—I don't share them with anyone."

He sighed, and some of his toughness seemed to disappear.

Closing his eyes, he leaned his head against the back of the sofa and said, "Everyone is entitled to privacy. I'm not trying to turn you inside out. I just need to know that I'm not in for any surprises."

"Such as?"

"Such as a husband or boyfriend who'll want to start throwing punches the next time he sees me."

"I already told you I wasn't married."

"No boyfriends at all?"

"Not currently."

He relaxed a bit. The lines around his mouth vanished. "Good. Another man would be hard to explain."

"You don't have to worry about that," she said, thinking fleetingly of Luke. She wondered if she should mention him, but decided against it. Luke was long gone—somewhere in Montana by now—and Valerie didn't want to think about him. Ever.

"Let's get started," Hale said, straightening. "Where did we meet? In Union Square? The Caribbean? At the office?"

"I don't know," she replied, already resenting her part in this deception. "I'll leave the lies to you."

"I'm not very good at lying."

"Then you should have come up with another idea."

"It's too late now," he said, his voice stone cold. "I already had our engagement announced in the papers."

"You *what*?"

"It'll be in the next edition."

"But you didn't even know I'd agree!" she gasped, outraged. She thought of her mother and the stack of newspapers at her bedside. Surely she would read the news!

"Of course I did. Everyone has a price."

Valerie wanted to argue the fact, but couldn't. He'd bought her, hadn't he? She shuddered inside. The ink on her employment agreement wasn't even dry and she was already second-guessing herself, wondering if she'd just made a deal with the devil himself.

# Chapter Three

Okay," Hale said, studying Shamus with a wary eye. "Other than what's written on your résumé and that you live here with this friendly guy—" he tried to pet the tabby's striped head, but Shamus backed away, hissed loudly, then streaked across the room to the French doors "—what else should I know about you?" He turned his attention from the cat to Valerie.

"You want to know my background," she murmured, feeling stripped bare under Hale's steady gaze. For something to do, she opened the doors to the balcony, and as the cat slunk out, a warm, moist breeze invaded the room.

"Right. All the high points. You can tell me on the way to dinner."

"Dinner?"

"And shopping," he said, starting for the door.

Things were moving much too quickly. "Shopping—for what?"

"An engagement ring for starters."

"No way! I'm not going to—"

"Sure you are," Hale cut in. "This has got to look convincing. And as far as the rest, you'll need clothes for the cruise."

"I have clothes."

He cast a glance toward her ridiculously small closet. "The Stowells dress for dinner every night—and I'm not talking about cutoff jeans and thongs. I mean they dress in formal attire. You'll need at least ten designer dresses—some evening gowns to start with—"

"Slow down," Valerie said. "I agreed to pretend to be your fiancée, but I didn't say I'd change anything about me."

"You'll have to fit in or Stowell will know something's up."

"Fit in?" she threw back at him. "I thought I was the perfect woman—the only one who would do."

"You are."

"Then you'll have to take me as I am, which is not, by the way, anything close to uppercrust. I'm just a working girl trying to make something of myself, and you and William Stowell and the rest of the world will have to accept it!"

Hale frowned, his brows forming a thick, single line across his forehead.

"You wanted the facts—well, you're going to get them," she went on, warming to her subject. "I was born in Phoenix, Arizona. My folks moved to L.A. when I was five and we stayed there until I was thirteen, when my father died of a heart attack. I don't have any brothers or sisters and I've never been married. I put myself through UCLA by taking small acting parts—mainly commercials—and modeling assignments. I graduated and landed a job at Liddell, but you know all about that—''

"Not all," he reminded her.

A blush, starting at the top of her shoulders, climbed up her neck and tinged her cheeks. Ignoring him, she said, "My mother's name is Anna Pryce. She lives here in San Francisco and is recovering from an accident in which some idiot plowed into her car with a huge pickup, then took off. He's never been found."

"Hit and run?"

"Yes," she said, cringing inside. "Fortunately she's recovering, but she's got a lot of time on her hands and she just happens to read the newspaper from the front page through the automobile ads. I doubt if she'll miss our engagement announcement."

"We can explain that."

"Can we? I just came from her apartment, where I told her that I didn't get the job at Donovan Enterprises. Her comment was that the guy that interviewed me wasn't too smart."

A crooked smile crept across his jaw. "I think I'd like to meet your mother."

"Don't worry, you'll get your chance." Angry with herself, she walked onto the balcony, where Shamus was perched on the rail, eyeing gray-and-white sea gulls that swooped and floated on the wind overhead.

Hearing Hale's footsteps behind her, she turned, squinting against the late-afternoon sunshine. "You know, Donovan, if we're going to play this game, we'd better do it right. Otherwise your web of lies might start untangling. Just think what might happen if my mother called the editor at the *Times*, told him he'd got his facts wrong and demanded an apology—in the paper?"

"She wouldn't."

"You don't know my mother." She tossed her hair over her shoulder. "And you don't know that William Stowell, or any of his family, doesn't read the society news. If the Stowells see a retraction, instigated by my mother—"

"You've made your point." He clamped his mouth shut.

"Good." Feeling the warm breeze tangle her hair and brush her cheeks, Valerie stared once again at the view. The noise of the city sounded distant, and the fragrant scent of roses from the planters on the deck wafted in the air. She thought about her mother—how hurt she would be that Valerie hadn't confided in her. "I think we'd better straighten things out with Mom, and fast."

"I already said I'd meet her."

"And charm the socks off her, right?"

"For starters."

Valerie didn't want to think about her mother's reaction to Hale. The way Valerie's luck was running, Anna Pryce would probably like the arrogant son-of-a-gun and welcome him as her future son-in-law! What a disaster that could be! "Listen, Hale, I don't want to lie to Mom."

"What's this—a latent sense of conscience?"

"She'll have to be told the truth," Valerie said, thinking aloud. Her mother deserved to know she had no intention of marrying a man like Hale Donovan.

"No way," he said, his smile fading. "I can't take the chance."

"Just my mother—no one else has to know."

His smile collapsed. "Do you think I'd go to all this trouble, then sabotage myself? It's only for a couple of weeks. Then, once the papers with Stowell are signed and we're back on land, you can tell her anything you want."

Valerie's eyes narrowed. "You really are a bastard. You know that, don't you?"

All kindness left his features. He jutted his jaw forward, and his eyes snapped with an inner fire. "Don't ever," he warned, his voice the barest of whispers, "call me that again." He strode swiftly back into the apartment and reached for her jacket, hanging on the brass tree near the door, then flung it at her as she followed him inside. "Let's go."

She caught her jacket on the fly. "I'm sorry if I—"

"Forget it."

Realizing she'd touched a raw nerve, she slipped into her shoes. "I didn't mean to offend you."

"You didn't," he shot back, waiting until she crossed the threshold, then closing the door firmly behind her.

"But—"

"Let's just pretend it didn't happen. Okay?"

Valerie tilted her chin up and met his angry gaze with her own. "It's forgotten, Hale," she said slowly, "but the next time I try to apologize, let me."

"Hopefully there won't be any reason to."

As she stood alone with him on the landing, the magnitude of what she'd agreed to do hit her full force. This man was handsome and powerful, and used to giving out orders that were instantly obeyed—no questions asked.

Mentally Valerie crossed her fingers. They'd only been together half an hour and already they were at each other's throats. How could they possibly spend two weeks cooped up on a boat together?

His car was parked three streets away, a sleek black Jaguar glinting beneath the late-afternoon sun. "My mother will never believe we're a couple," Valerie said, eyeing the car as he unlocked the door for her.

"Why not?"

"I took a solemn oath never to date a guy with an expensive car."

His dark expression lightened as he slid behind the wheel. "Strange vow, isn't it?"

"Call it self-preservation."

With a flick of his wrist, the powerful engine thrummed to life. "Why?"

"Most of the boys in college who drove around in flashy cars turned out to be self-centered, egotistical jerks."

"That's a pretty broad statement."

She shrugged slightly as he eased into traffic. "I suppose."

"And prejudiced." He shifted, putting the Jag through its paces. Fresh air, filled with the salty scent of the sea, blew in through a partially opened window. "Where did you learn to be so cynical?"

"Seems like a natural progression," she said, staring out the window and trying to block out the image of Luke that invariably came to mind. Luke, blond and tanned by the southern California sun, with an all-American face and roving eye. Proud owner of a flashy red Porsche and a surfer's body honed to perfection. The quintessential boy who refused to grow up—the only man Valerie had ever come close to loving.

She felt the weight of Hale's gaze upon her and forced a smile. "So—what are we going to tell my mother?"

"I've been working on that," he said, cranking on the wheel. As they drove down the hilly streets, Valerie could see the sparkling waters of the bay, dark blue and shimmering. Sea gulls flew overhead, and boats sliced through the water, leaving frothy wakes.

Hale parked near Ghiradelli Square, a former chocolate factory, which was positioned on the hill overlooking the bay. The series of brick-faced buildings had been renovated and now housed a maze of shops and restaurants.

He helped her from the car, then took her hand and guided her up a flight of exterior stairs. Olive trees, flower beds and benches were interspersed between buildings with such names as Mustard Building, Power House or Cocoa Building. Shoppers and sightseers browsed through the alleys. Birds chirped and flitted from the shrubs to the walkways.

"This isn't the way to my mother's, you know," Valerie said as they passed a mermaid fountain.

"Isn't it?"

"What're we doing here?"

He opened the double-oak-and-glass doors of an Irish restaurant tucked into a shaded corner of the square. "This is my favorite place in the city," he explained.

The smells of spices and smoke filled a cozy restaurant with bare, glossy tables, glass-encased candles and a long bar of dark wood inlaid with brass. The bar had no stools, and patrons bellied up to it and rested their feet on a genuine brass rail. Behind the polished wood, mirrors rose to a fifteen-foot ceiling. Green, brown and clear bottles were reflected in the glass.

The sounds of laughter and whispered conversation drifted over the hum of lazy paddle fans mounted high overhead. Hale didn't wait to be seated, but tugged on Valerie's hand and led her to a corner booth with a view of the street below.

"You're a regular," she guessed.

"You could say that."

A waiter appeared as they sat, and brought two frosted glasses of hearty Irish ale.

"I don't get a choice?" Valerie asked as the waiter disappeared between the closely packed tables.

Hale grinned across his mug. "Consider it an initiation rite."

"One that all your fiancées go through?"

Winking broadly, he settled back in his chair and eyed her over the frosted lip of his mug. "I've never been engaged before."

"What happened? Didn't you offer enough money?"

He lifted one corner of his mouth. "I guess not—until now."

"So who else have you initiated?"

"Most of the women I've dated have been here at one time or another."

"Oh." She couldn't hide the disappointment in her voice and wondered why it was there. What did it matter if Hale had brought dozens of other women in here? This was all just an act—nothing more. To hide her feelings, she picked up the menu. "Do I get to choose my own meal?"

"I'll work on it, but it might be tough. The guy who owns this place, Tim Buchanan, is an old fraternity brother of mine. When he hears that we're here, he'll probably—" Hale glanced over her shoulder, and his grin widened "—well, speak of the devil."

"About time you showed your ugly mug around here, Donovan!" Tim Buchanan moved lithely between the tables. Over six feet tall, crowned with a thatch of blazing red hair that matched his neatly clipped beard, he wore a crisp white shirt, black slacks and bow tie. His face was dusted with freckles, and small blue eyes peered fondly at Hale. He reached across the table and clasped Hale's hand in a grip that looked positively punishing.

"And who's this?" he asked, turning his attention to Valerie.

"Valerie Pryce... Tim Buchanan. Valerie's my fiancée."

Tim's smile froze. He turned his head abruptly, and his gaze landed back on Hale. "The devil you say! You? Married?" He turned back to Valerie, and a small smile played beneath his red beard. "Well, you've got yourself a handful, that you do, Ms. Pryce. If this guy ever gets out of line, you call on me!"

"Oh, I won't need any help, but thank you very much," she said with a heartfelt sigh. "Hale's just an angel. Anything I want and—" she shrugged her slim shoulders and lifted a palm "—there it is!" With what she hoped was an adoring expression on her face, she turned to Hale. "Isn't that right, darling?"

"An angel?" Tim hooted, and the back of Hale's neck burned scarlet. "Donovan? Wait till I tell Father O'Flannery!"

"Who's he?" Valerie asked innocently, though she could sense Hale squirming in his chair.

"Who's he? The man who personally acquainted Hale with the wrath of God." Laughing loudly, Tim turned, signaled to the bartender and said, "A round on the house—my best friend is getting married!"

The men at the bar cheered, and Hale sank lower in his seat. Tim wasn't finished. "Dinner's on me—the house specialty!"

"Hey, you don't have to—"

Tim cut off Hale's protest with an impatient wave. "It's not every day you walk in here and announce you're getting married. I'll be back in a minute."

Still chuckling, he headed through swinging doors that Valerie assumed led to the kitchen.

"What the hell was that all about?" Hale demanded, the skin on his face stretched taut. "'Angel,' my eye!"

"I just thought you should know what we're going to be in for," she replied, enjoying herself. It was time he found out this charade wasn't going to be a bed of roses. "The next couple of weeks aren't going to be easy on either of us."

"What does it matter? You're being paid—and very well."

"Then you'll want me to continue to play the part of adoring wife-to-be, right?"

Hale frowned. "Just don't overdo it."

"Wouldn't dream of it, darling," she replied, her hazel eyes twinkling mischievously as Tim brought back two steaming platters of crawfish smothered in a spicy brown sauce, spinach salads with lemon and bacon and a bottle of champagne.

"May as well do this right," Tim said as he uncorked the bottle. The cork popped, frothy champagne slid down the long neck of the bottle, and Tim poured three glasses, holding his aloft. "To the years ahead," he said solemnly, "life, love, happiness and fertility!"

Hale nearly choked.

Valerie laughed out loud.

And Tim, smirking, winked at his friend, then gulped his drink. "About time you took the plunge," he said before slapping Hale on the shoulder and heading back to the kitchen.

"I thought you weren't going to overdo it," Hale reminded her, jabbing at his salad with his fork.

"I'm trying not to, believe me," she said, but felt the cat-who-ate-the-canary grin spreading across her face.

"Just don't push me," he warned.

"Wouldn't dream of it, 'darling.'" She touched the rim of her glass to his. "Here's to the next two weeks."

"May they pass quickly," he muttered.

"Amen!" She sipped from her glass, enjoying the feel of the champagne as it bubbled in her throat. Hale refilled her glass several times, but she didn't care. The tip of her nose grew numb, and she felt the unlikely urge to smile giddily. And most unnerving of all, she couldn't take her eyes off Hale. What would it be like to really be in love with him? she wondered as she studied his strong chin, his thin, sensual lips, his deep-set, and brooding eyes.

"Irish coffee?" Tim asked when he returned for their empty plates.

"And dessert—chocolate mousse?" Hale suggested, glancing at her for approval.

"I couldn't—I'm stuffed," she whispered.

Tim lifted one brawny shoulder. "Then I'll bring one serving with two spoons."

"Just like in a 1950s soda shop," Valerie said with a giggle.

Hale shot a murderous glance in her direction.

"Right—for lovebirds," Tim agreed, chuckling.

A muscle worked in Hale's jaw. Valerie thought he might explode and tell his friend the engagement was all an act, but instead, to her mortification, he reached across the table and grabbed her hand, stroking the back of her fingers with one thumb. "Then again, maybe we don't have time for dessert or coffee," he said huskily, his gray eyes smoldering with unspoken desire. "We've got better things to do."

Valerie blushed and felt her mouth turn to cotton. Licking suddenly dry lips, she jerked back her hand.

"Well, don't let me hold you up," Tim said, sending Hale a knowing look as he was called back to the bar.

"That was unnecessary!" Valerie hissed as Hale, taking her elbow in a proprietary grip, propelled her out of the restaurant.

"You asked for it."

"I did no such—"

"Oh, come on, you were really working me over in front of Tim. And you enjoyed every minute of it!"

She couldn't argue. She had felt a perverse satisfaction at making him squirm. There was something about knocking Hale Donovan down a peg that she couldn't resist. "Okay, okay," she agreed as he elbowed open the door, "maybe we should start over—with a truce."

He raised a cynical dark brow, and his hand never left her arm as he guided her through the crowds in the square, around a corner and up a short flight of steps. "A truce—you think that's possible?"

"Probably not, but it's the only way we're going to survive the next two weeks."

"Agreed." He offered her a roguish smile that caused her heart to trip unexpectedly. "Now before the store closes..." Still holding her arm, he shoved open the door of a jewelry shop. A small bell tinkled as they crossed the threshold.

"Mr. Donovan!" A reed-thin woman with thick dark hair pinned away from her face glanced up, smiled and quickly closed the glass case where she'd been arranging bracelets. She hurried across the small shop to greet Hale. In heels, she was nearly as tall as Hale, and her suit, a rich red silk, rustled as she stretched out a slender hand. "What can I do for you today?"

"We need a ring—a diamond."

The woman raised her finely arched eyebrows a fraction. "A cocktail ring?"

"Engagement."

"Oh." She sounded vaguely disappointed as she moved over to a glass case where diamonds of every description were displayed in open, velvet-lined boxes.

"This is my fiancée, Valerie Pryce."

"My best wishes," the woman murmured.

"Thank you," Valerie ground out.

"Now what kind of diamond would you like?"

"Nothing too flashy, just a nice stone without a lot of frills." Hale glanced at Valerie. "That okay with you?"

"It doesn't really matter to me, remember? I'm not all that crazy about being here in the first place."

The saleslady did her best to keep her expression bland, but Valerie could read the questions in her eyes—a million of them.

Hale shot Valerie a warning look, then asked to see the ring.

"Any special cut?" the saleslady asked. "Square? Pear-shaped?"

"How about that one?" Hale pointed to a ring near the front of the case, and Valerie had to bite her tongue. The setting and stone were gorgeous.

With great care, the woman pulled out a gold ring crowned by a winking marquis-cut stone and slipped it on Valerie's ring finger. The diamond looked huge—not gawdy, by any means, but still it felt like a deadweight on her hand.

"It'll need to be adjusted—just a little, but I can have that done while you wait—"

"Fine," Hale said. "Charge it to my account."

"Will do."

Valerie handed the ring back to the saleslady, who walked crisply to the back of the store. "Don't you think you're pushing this too far? What're you going to do with that ring when this is all over?"

"I haven't thought that far ahead."

"I don't believe you. I think you've thought this all out very carefully." She studied him through narrowed eyes. "But you really don't have to buy that ring. Can't you just rent one or buy an imitation?"

"And have you appear cheap to the Stowells?" he mocked. "No way. This has got to be the real thing."

"You must want Stowell's company very badly."

"I do."

"And it doesn't matter what it costs or that you have to lie in order to get it?"

"It's worth it."

"So it all comes down to money, right?"

"Doesn't everything?" he asked.

Valerie wanted to ask him about love and happiness, but she bit her tongue. The man was obviously jaded. He thought money could buy him everything he wanted or needed in life, and maybe it could. It had bought her, hadn't it?

As she watched him move impatiently from one glass case to the next, she realized he was a man who didn't believe in love and didn't have time for it. He was too busy amassing his next million to get involved in anything as complicated as love.

Within minutes the saleslady reappeared, wearing a satisfied smile. "Here we go—let's see if this is any better." She tried the ring on Valerie again and it fitted perfectly, the bright stone catching the light.

"Great," Hale said.

"It's a beautiful ring," the saleswoman agreed as she motioned to another case. "Could I interest you in a necklace or earrings—"

"No!" Valerie said quickly.

Hale grinned wickedly. "Not right now, but we'll think about them."

"Do." The saleslady pressed a card into his hand. "Just give me a call. And congratulations."

Valerie didn't say a word all the way back to the car. This engagement thing was getting totally out of hand.

"You don't like the ring," Hale said as he slipped the Jaguar into the tangle of early-evening traffic.

She slid a glance in his direction and noticed the smile toying at his lips. Damn the man, he was enjoying this. "The ring's beautiful. It's the sentiment that bothers me."

"Don't worry about it."

"I'll try not to. All part of the deal, right?"

"Right." He grimaced tightly as he shifted down. "Okay, so where does your mother live?"

Valerie rattled off the address, and Hale turned south. "Have you come up with a plausible story yet?" she wondered aloud. "Mom will ask a ton of questions."

"How about the truth? You fell hopelessly in love with me and threw yourself at my feet."

Valerie smothered a smile. "Oh, that'll work."

"Or maybe you're after my money—that's closer to the truth."

"You're pushing it, Donovan."

"'Honey,' remember? From now on it's 'honey.'"

"Oh, right." Good Lord, what had she gotten herself into? "Well, 'honey,' you'd better come up with a good story, because Mom will expect one."

"By all means."

She settled back in the Jaguar and watched him from the corner of her eye. A handsome, intelligent man, he showed a spark of humor, which softened the hard edge of his arrogance.

"How about we met at the beach a few weeks ago, but we kept our affair—"

"No affair. This is my *mother*, remember?"

He slid a questioning glance in her direction. "This isn't the Victorian era."

Valerie stared straight ahead. "Not to you, maybe, but my mother and I *don't* discuss my sex life. Let's keep it that way."

"Whatever you say."

"Good. Now, what's our story?" She cringed inside. This was getting more complicated by the minute. Sighing, she leaned back in her seat. Maybe after the first lie, it would get easier.

"How about this," Hale suggested. "We kept the fact that we were in love a secret because we wanted to be sure of our feelings before we told the world we'd found each other."

Rolling her eyes, Valerie muttered, "This sounds like a story line for *Life's Golden Sands.*"

At that he looked perplexed.

"It's a soap opera, the one on which I played a minor part for six months—a fact you'd better remember if you want to pull this off. I was Tess, the tortured stepdaughter of rich Trevor Billings, who's natural son was always coming on to me—"

"Enough! Spare me all the grisly details," Hale growled. "I get the idea."

He found a parking space within two blocks of the apartment building, and before Valerie could catch her breath, she was letting herself into her mother's second-story unit.

"Val? That you?" her mother called.

"Yep! And I brought a...friend." She closed the door behind Hale and saw her mother seated on the living room couch, an open book on her lap. Valerie took a deep breath. "Mom, I'd like you to meet Hale Donovan."

"The man who...?"

Stuffing her hands into her pockets, Valerie said, "The man who wouldn't hire me. And there's a reason for that—"

"I'm in love with your daughter, Mrs. Pryce," Hale said, stepping forward and placing his arm possessively across Valerie's shoulders. "And we have a strict policy at Donovan Enterprises. We don't allow close relatives to work together. That goes for the boss, too."

"But...? Val?" her mother asked, confused.

Valerie felt horrid. "I think I should explain—"

Hale cut her off. "I've asked your daughter to be my wife and she's accepted," he said to her mother. The words sounded so sincere Valerie nearly believed him.

Anna Pryce's mouth dropped open. "You're getting married?" Her gaze, clouded with suspicion, flicked from Valerie to Hale and back again.

"Yes."

"When?" she asked, stunned.

"Soon," Hale said vaguely.

"Now wait a minute." Anna shoved her book aside and pinned her daughter with her unconvinced stare. "Why is this the first I've heard of it?"

"It, uh, is sudden," Valerie offered lamely.

"That's the understatement of the century." Anna's eyes snapped. "Now let's start all over. At the beginning. And don't tell me the beginning happened between this afternoon and this evening, because I just won't believe it. What's going on here?''

Valerie swallowed hard. She'd always been a lousy liar. "Look, Mom," she said, sitting on the couch and touching her mother's arm. "I should have told you all about this sooner, I guess, but we just decided to make our engagement official this afternoon.''

"After you left here," her mother clarified.

"Right. And I know it's kind of a shock.''

"A big shock.''

"Right—I know, but I just want you to trust me on this, okay?" She took her mother's hands between her own.

"Marriage is a big step.''

"Mom, I'm twenty-four.''

"And you almost made a mistake once before, remember?''

From the corner of her eye, Valerie saw Hale's muscles stiffen. "That was a long time ago.''

"So now two years is a long time—''

"Mom, please. Believe me, I know what I want.''

Anna sighed tiredly and pinched her eyebrows into a suspicious frown. "I guess I don't have much choice, do I? You've always been a stubborn thing.''

"Amen," Hale whispered.

"We won't rush into anything," Valerie promised, shooting him a warning glance.

"Good," her mother replied.

There was more she wanted to say—a lot more. Valerie could sense it.

Feeling guilty, Valerie said, "I do have one favor to ask you. Hale and I are going on a cruise—just up the coast with some friends and business associates of his.'' To her surprise, her mother didn't bat an eye. She was probably still in shock. "Would you mind taking care of Shamus for a couple of weeks?"

"That beast? He hates me."

"And you adore him."

Anna glanced at Valerie's left hand, where the diamond glittered mockingly. "Of course I will," she said gently, though her forehead was still creased. "But when you get back, let's talk. I mean, really talk."

"We will," Valerie promised, wondering how she could tell her mother that everything she'd said was a bald-faced lie.

# Chapter Four

Did I pass inspection?" Hale asked once they were back in his car. He slid the Jaguar into gear and pulled into traffic. The sun, leaving a blaze of gold and magenta in its wake, had settled into the Pacific.

Valerie shook her head. "If you're asking if my mom bought our story, I think the answer is no. But she's going along with it just to humor me. And that's the point, isn't it?"

"Exactly."

Valerie leaned back in her seat, and as dusk settled, the interior of the car seemed smaller still—more intimate. Hale's carved features were shadowed with the coming night. His jaw appeared even stronger, his eyes more deep set, his lips thin, nearly cruel.

She noticed his hands on the steering wheel, large and strong. And his legs, with the fabric of his jeans pulling taut over his thighs, were dangerously close to hers. Swallowing uncomfortably, she fidgeted with the strap of her purse and shifted away from him, pressing her right side against the passenger door to assure her as much space as possible between his body and hers, then forced her gaze to the windshield.

She wasn't usually uncomfortable around men, but Hale had a way of making her restless; his sidelong glances were unnerving, his innate sexuality impossible to ignore.

He found a parking space not far from her apartment house and walked with her to the front door.

"You don't have to come up," she said as she twisted her key in the lock and felt the dead bolt give way.

"No," he drawled, "I suppose I don't." Leaning one shoulder against the door, he studied her for several heart-stopping seconds. "But we still have a lot of work to do. Your mother was just the first hurdle, you know."

"But a biggie."

Hale smiled, and in the night his flash of white teeth seemed genuine. It touched a spot in her heart she had thought no longer existed—a spot Luke had destroyed.

Suddenly she wanted to know all about Hale. "What about your family? Won't you have to tell them anything?"

His smile faded as quickly as it had appeared. "I don't have any family."

"None?" she said.

"My folks are both dead."

"I'm sorry—"

"It happened a long time ago. I don't really remember them. There's nothing for you to be sorry about," he clipped.

"But don't you have any brothers or sisters or cousins?"

"None." Under the twin bulbs mounted over the doors, his black hair gleamed and his eyes turned stone-cold.

"I didn't mean to pry," Valerie said quickly, embarrassed, "but I think I should know a little about you, too. If the Stowells are going to believe I'm engaged to you, it would only make sense that I know your history—at least part of it."

He took a few seconds to answer. "I suppose you're right."

"Well, I'd look pretty stupid if I showed up on the yacht and all I knew about the man I intended to spend the rest of my life with was that he owned an investment company."

He shrugged and held the door open for her. "You're right. I'll fill you in tomorrow morning."

"What're we doing tomorrow?"

He laughed, and started down the steps. "You'll find out then," he said, his voice filled with amusement as she shut the door behind him and turned the key.

Climbing the three steep flights, she wondered if she'd made a colossal mistake linking up with someone as unpredictable as Hale Donovan. Surprisingly, she felt lighthearted at the prospect of seeing him again, and that bothered her. It bothered her a lot.

The next morning Valerie yanked every garment she owned from her closet and tossed each piece onto her open daybed. She had small piles of skirts, dresses, blouses, jackets, sweaters and slacks, all very tailored and nice enough, though nothing extravagant or particularly expensive.

"So who cares?" she muttered, staring at an even more dismal stack of jeans, shorts and T-shirts. Shamus hopped onto the bed and settled between two of the piles. "Thank you, but I don't think I need cat hair all over my wardrobe." Gently she lifted the fat tabby and stroked his silky head. "So what d'ya think? Will I pass as the illustrious Hale Donovan's bride?"

Shamus yawned, scrambled out of her arms and flopped on the floor where the sunlight filtered through the window to warm the old oak boards.

"Yeah, a lot of help you are," she mumbled, realizing as she sorted through her clothes and came up with a few suitable outfits that Hale had been right. She didn't have much in the way of yachting attire—and she didn't really care.

She packed two sun dresses, a couple of pairs of slacks and matching sweaters, then tossed her favorite pair of jeans and her only decent shorts into her suitcase. As an afterthought she found her one silk blouse, added it to the case and sorted through her shoes. After organizing her meager wardrobe, she flipped on the coffee maker.

Ten minutes later the doorbell rang, and Shamus, a streak of greased lightning, made a beeline for the open French doors.

Valerie checked the peephole, saw Hale's handsome face and braced herself. Dealing with Hale reminded her of going into battle. Unlatching the door, she asked, "Are you always this prompt?"

"A habit I can't break." He strode into the room, slapped a newspaper onto the table, then smiling, surveyed the mess on the bed. "Packing?"

"If you can call it that."

He motioned to the suitcase. "Need anything?"

"Nothing I can't buy myself."

"You're sure about that?" To her mortification, he walked over to her open case and took stock. "Where's the rest?"

"The rest of what?"

"Your other bags—and trunk."

"I don't have any other bags. I thought I'd pick up a few more things and that would be it."

"This isn't an overnight camp-out on the beach, you know."

Valerie bristled. "And *you* know that I'm not going to pretend I'm some kind of rich debutante. I don't have that kind of money and I think I'm a few years too old. I'm a working girl, I come from middle-class roots, and if William Stowell doesn't like it, he can damn well lump it!"

Hale's mouth twitched.

"I don't think he'll care where I came from as long as you convince him that you're involved with me and that you're not interested in his daughter or her money."

His head snapped up. He dropped her clothes. "Her money?"

"That is what this is all about, isn't it? You've got to prove I've got the money behind me to keep you interested. Otherwise Stowell won't believe that Hale Donovan, who worships the almighty dollar above all else, is seriously going to marry me!"

"That wasn't the reason."

"No—then what was?" she demanded, crossing the room to stand so close to him she could smell his cologne, see the flecks of blue in his steel-gray eyes.

"I just wanted you to feel like you fitted in."

"Don't worry about me. I'll be fine."

"If you say so."

"I'm positive," she said, angling her face up to his defiantly. "You chose me, Donovan, so I expect you to take me as I am."

"It's 'honey,' not 'Donovan,' remember?" A twinge of a smile tugged at his lips.

"This is all a big joke to you, isn't it?"

"I don't joke when business is involved," he said, "but I think we may as well enjoy ourselves as much as possible. We can spend the next couple of weeks pretending to like each other in front of everyone and lunging for each other's throats when we're alone, or we can try to get along. I think you were the one who suggested a 'truce.'"

"Call me an idealist," she mocked, but smiled in spite of herself.

"Let me pour you a cup of coffee," he suggested, opening first one cupboard, then the next, until he found two ceramic mugs labeled UCLA. "From college?"

"Umm." Not only from college, but from Luke. The first gift he'd ever given her. She felt her face drain of color, but accepted a cup and sipped gratefully.

"We made page one of the society section," Hale announced, then poured another cup for himself.

Valerie's stomach dropped as she flipped open the newspaper he'd brought in with him. On the first page of the society section in bold black letters, the headline read: DONOVAN TO WED.

"Oh, great," she whispered, scanning the article, which listed her name, that she was a graduate of UCLA and a resident of San Francisco. Other than that, she was fairly anonymous. The article stated that no date had been picked for the wedding, then went on to sketch out a little of Hale's success in business. "It's not too bad," she admitted.

"A little on the vague side," he said, "but it covers all the bases."

"Don't you mean it covers your backside—as far as Stowell is concerned."

"That, too." Hale took a swallow and gulped, nearly sputtering. "What *is* this stuff?"

Valerie wasn't in the mood to be razzed about her coffee. With a sweet smile she didn't feel, she said, "It's a mild decaffeinated Colombian blend mixed with Viennese mocha."

"Well, it's horrible."

"Thanks a lot—it's my special brew."

"Yeah, well, it needs work—like a complete overhaul."

She lifted her brows innocently. "Then it's a good thing we're not really getting married, or you'd have to live with it."

"Nope. I'd make the coffee. Come on, I'll take you out for a real breakfast."

She should have been angry, she supposed. His high-handedness was uncalled for. But the dimple in his cheek and the glint in his eyes convinced her he'd only been teasing. "Breakfast and then what?" she asked, locking Shamus inside.

"Whatever the day brings."

"Is this the surprise you told me about?"

"The first of many," he said with a laugh.

Outside, the morning fog was beginning to burn off. Wisps still hung over the water, but most of the hilly city was exposed to the August sun's warm rays.

Hale drove down the steep streets to the waterfront, where they took a ferry north across San Francisco Bay to Tiburon. There they left the Jaguar and stood on the upper deck of the boat, near the prow. Salt spray filled

Valerie's nostrils with the scent of the sea, and the wind was strong enough to burn her cheeks. The water was clear and smooth, and she had to shout to Hale to be heard over the heavy drone of the ferry's huge engines.

Hale didn't touch her, but stood close, the breeze ruffling his hair as they passed Alcatraz, stopped at Angel Island, headed north again and finally docked at Tiburon.

Hale drove into the town and parked in a parking lot near the waterfront.

Valerie slipped out of the car, and felt warm rays of the sun beat against her crown. Hale took her hand, and though she was surprised, she didn't protest, but followed as he guided her along a cement walkway to the docks and a tiny café perched over the water.

His fingers felt strong and warm, and despite the fact that his touch wasn't the least bit intimate, Valerie felt her pulse accelerate.

He shoved open the door, and a small bell tinkled. Spying Hale, a plump waitress with freckles and short-cropped brown hair snatched a couple of menus and smiled broadly. "Well, Mr. Donovan," she said with a grin. "Long time no see."

"Hi, Rose. It has been a while."

"Well, don't make yourself such a stranger." Her bright gaze rested on Valerie, and as they walked through a back door to a covered patio, Hale made introductions.

"I read where you were finally tying the big one," Rose said. "High time."

"Mmm," Hale replied noncommittally.

Rose handed Valerie a menu. "You're a lucky lady," she said, pouring water for each of them as the doorbell chimed again. "I'll be back for your order in a minute."

"Another fraternity brother?" Valerie asked once Rose was out of sight.

"Very funny."

"Why did we come all the way over here for breakfast?" she asked.

"Atmosphere, for one thing."

The small café had plenty of that. The few tables scattered over the flagstones were shaded by a trellis over which fragrant lilacs blossomed in purple clusters. Beyond the porch was a path leading to the dock and an open view to the bay, where gleaming yachts plowed through the blue water.

"Tomorrow we'll be boarding *The Regina*—"

"The what?"

"Stowell named his boat after his daughter."

"Oh."

"I thought you'd like a sneak preview. After breakfast we'll go down to the dock and I'll point her out to you."

A cold knot tightened in Valerie's stomach. Until that moment she hadn't really thought about sailing away with Hale—or what fourteen days cooped up with him could do to her. In just twenty-four hours he'd managed to unnerve her. What would happen in two weeks?

"Have you decided?" Rose asked, breezing back to the patio, notepad poised and ready.

"Oh, uh, sure . . ." Valerie scanned the menu quickly. "A Belgian waffle with strawberries."

"I'll have the seafood omelet," Hale said, then winked at Valerie. Her heart did a ridiculous somersault. "And a cup of coffee. Real coffee."

* * *

An hour later they walked to the dock and watched several magnificent white vessels sail through the water. Huge yachts raced against smaller sleek sailboats.

"Stowell's boat is moored at the yacht club, one of the closest berths." Squinting against the sun, Hale stood behind Valerie and pointed, resting his arm lightly on her shoulder. "It's one of the largest—see."

"They're all large," she said, slipping sunglasses onto her nose and following the extended path of his finger. Shining white vessels, their masts and rigging outlined against the blue horizon, swayed gently on the water. Smaller sloops were moored next to larger cutters, ketches and schooners.

"I could take you over and introduce you today."

"I'd just as soon wait until tomorrow."

He slanted her a lazy smile and linked his arm through hers. "Chicken."

"That's me," she said with a laugh.

"I think you'll like the Stowells."

"Will I?" she asked, then shrugged. "I like most people."

"I thought maybe I'd scared you off—all the talk about their money—and their daughter."

"I won't hold it against them that they're rich, if that's what you mean."

His smile widened. "You know, Ms. Pryce, if we try, we might just enjoy ourselves on this trip."

She doubted it. Two weeks cooped up with Hale while he was trying to negotiate a business deal? What would she do? Chitchat with Regina—a woman with whom she had nothing in common. Nothing, that was, except for Hale Donovan? Yep, it sounded like a rip-roaring good time already. She could hardly wait.

Lost in thought, Valerie slid into the sunbaked interior of Hale's Jaguar. She watched as Hale tossed his jacket behind the front seat and shoved his shirtsleeves over his tanned forearms. An interesting man, Hale Donovan, she thought as they drove through a dusty parking lot and turned toward highway 101.

Small drops of perspiration collected at her hairline, and she rested her arm on the open window, surprised at how at ease she felt with a man she barely knew. He reached into the glove compartment, found a pair of mirrored aviator sunglasses and shoved them on his nose.

"You promised to tell me something about yourself," she finally said.

"What do you want to know?"

"Everything, I suppose."

"I graduated from Berkeley ten years ago, worked for someone else for a while and saved some money. I bought a company that was going bankrupt, for a song, turned it around, made a profit, bought another company the next year and just kept buying and expanding."

"The man with the Midas touch."

"I wish," he muttered, adjusting his glasses.

"What about your personal life?"

"I don't have time for one."

"But there have been women," she hinted.

"Not many."

"No?" Men as wealthy and handsome as Donovan usually had women crawling all over them.

"If there were women—or at least one woman—I wouldn't have had to find a stranger to pull off this charade, now would I?" he asked flippantly, his jaw clenched.

"What about your friends?"

"You met Tim. I have a few others. Most of them work for me."

"Your *friends* are your employees?"

"Some of them. Some of the people who work for me don't like me much." He cranked hard on the wheel and turned south, toward San Francisco. "Anything else you want to know?"

"Where did you go to high school?"

Was it her imagination, or did he flinch? She couldn't see his eyes, hidden as they were behind his glasses, but she felt a sudden coldness invade the car's interior. "I went to a private school in Oakland. It's not important. Stowell won't expect you to know anything about it."

"But if the subject comes up—"

"Change it!"

"Aye, aye, Captain," she shot back, irritated at his dictatorial tone. "Since we obviously can't talk about your personal life," she went on, unable to hold her tongue, "why don't you tell me about your business? Good ol' Donovan Enterprises. Weren't you in trouble with the IRS a couple of years ago?"

Now he really did flinch. "A couple accounting errors. We cleared them up."

"Then there was that takeover of some oil leases—"

"That was straightened out by the attorneys. What's the point, Valerie?"

"I just want a feel for the company I'm going to be working for."

"A little late for that, isn't it?"

"Maybe not. There've been rumors that Donovan Enterprises walks a thin line with the law."

"Is that why you wanted a job with us?" he mocked.

"Look, I needed a job. It's that simple. You pay well and offer a good chance for advancement."

He twisted his mouth in a sarcastic grin. "So to hell with our ethics, is that it? You know, Ms. Pryce, if I didn't know better, I'd think you might be an opportunist."

"That's a little like the pot calling the kettle black."

"If the shoe fits—"

"Enough with the clichés," she muttered, but couldn't help grinning.

"Then I'm to assume you're through assassinating my character?"

"For the time being." She stared through the windshield. The Golden Gate Bridge loomed ahead, spanning the neck of the bay and leading across clear, sun-dappled water to the city. Hale drove straight to Fisherman's Wharf, searched for a parking spot and settled for a place several blocks away.

"Come on," he said, climbing out of the car.

"What're we doing here?"

"Consider it part of your training." He drew his lips into a smug smile, and though she couldn't see his eyes behind those sunglasses, she guessed he was laughing at her.

They spent several hours wandering through the docks, eyeing fresh produce and seafood, trinkets and souvenirs. They walked slowly with the tourists crowding the sidewalk. The sounds of voices and automobile engines and the pungent scents of fresh fish and salt air, all mingled in the warm afternoon.

Hale stopped at several spots, buying cooked crab and smoked salmon at one fish market, a loaf of crusty French bread and scones at a small bakery and two bottles of Chianti from a tiny shop that specialized in local wines.

"Now what?" Valerie asked, laughing as they walked up the few blocks to the Jaguar.

"Now we go to my place."

"Your place?" she repeated, her smile falling from her face and her confidence slipping.

"Scared?"

*Yes!* "Of course not, but I don't see why—"

"Because to make our story believable you'll have to know where and how I live, right?"

"There's no reason—"

"The Stowells have been to my house. All of them. Come on. I won't bite. I promise."

She racked her brain for a logical excuse. Though she knew it was childish, she wasn't ready to be alone with him in the privacy of his home—not yet. "I have to finish packing tonight."

"We won't be late."

"I guess I don't have much of a choice."

"Just consider it part of the job."

And the job was making her more uneasy by the minute, Valerie thought ruefully.

Once they were inside the car, he drove southwest and up the steep, winding tree-lined streets of Pacific Heights.

Hale's house was an old renovated Victorian. With a brick facade and four full stories, the narrow house was taller than the maple trees in the small front yard.

Inside, oak floors gleamed with a warm patina and thick Oriental carpets in shades of blue and peach lay in each downstairs room. The furniture was arranged strategically, and watercolors, largely of seascapes, adorned the walls.

The original carved woodwork had been restored, and a splendid fireplace comprised an entire wall in both the living and the dining room. Chandeliers hung from the ceilings, and antique tables were placed around expensive, modern pieces in cream-colored leather.

"Eclectic," Valerie murmured.

"Interior by Elaine," he said, eyeing the rooms clinically as he led her to the back of the house. "She's a decorator a friend recommended to me."

In the kitchen were gleaming marble counters, and brass kettles hung from a wrought-iron rack suspended from the ceiling and balanced above a cooking island with a gas range. The cupboards had leaded glass inlays, and the floor was shiny tile.

"A gourmet's dream."

He acted as if he didn't care, as if he barely noticed his own kitchen. Setting his bags on the counter, he glanced around, pulled off his sunglasses and grinned a little sheepishly. "I'm hardly ever here. I have an apartment at the office. So when I work late..." He shrugged. "Doesn't seem to make much sense to drive all the way over here."

He showed her the rest of the house, a weight room, bath and study on the third floor and on the fourth a loft that housed the master bedroom. Complete with sloped ceilings and skylights, the bedroom stretched from the front of the house to the back. Buff-colored carpet covered the floors, and the brass bed was draped with a forest-green quilt that matched the fabric of the drapes. Yet another fireplace was nestled between cherry-wood bookcases, and a cluster of burgundy-colored chairs filled one corner.

"Don't tell me," Valerie said, eyeing the color-coordinated pieces and artfully arranged potted plants. "Elaine again."

"Bingo." Hale laughed, and the sound echoed against the high ceilings overhead.

"Does she put your suits and ties together, too?"

"That I handle on my own."

"I'm relieved to hear it."

"Are you?" he asked, and his gray eyes glinted suggestively.

"Of course I am," she said, refusing to lick her lips, though she suddenly felt nervous. "It's nice to know a thirty-year-old man can do a few things for himself."

"More than a few." His voice had lowered an octave.

"I'd hope so." Her skin tingled a little.

Leaning a hip against the rail surrounding the stairs, he crossed his arms over his chest. The fabric of his shirt was stretched tight, pulling at the seams. "You really do push it, don't you?"

"Push what?"

"Me, for one thing. But I suspect that you push and push and just keep pushing in everything you do."

"Not a bad attribute for an employee."

"But a decided fault in a wife."

"I'm not going to be your wife. Remember?"

"Just be careful—around the Stowells."

"On my best behavior," she mocked, lifting her hand. "Scout's honor."

Before she could react, he reached forward and clasped his fingers around her wrist. "This Stowell deal is important to me."

"So you've said."

"Don't blow it."

"Oh, I won't, 'sugar,'" she replied tartly, and saw him wince at the sarcastic tone of her endearment, "because it's important to me, as well."

He didn't release her, just stared straight into her eyes. Though she wanted to shrink away, she met his gaze with all the willpower she possessed. She thought she felt a change in the room temperature as he pressed his fingertips against the sensitive skin inside her wrist. Her pulse fairly fluttered and her heart was slamming against the inside of her ribs, but she managed to keep her hands steady.

"Just so we understand each other," he whispered, his voice husky and raw.

"Oh, I'm sure we do." She inched her chin up mutinously. "Now if the tour's over, maybe we should end this for tonight. I'll call a cab."

"Before dinner?"

"I didn't know I was staying."

"Consider it part of the job."

"Are you trying to make this unpleasant?" she asked, wishing she could think of a way to get out of staying longer. Lingering in his bedroom was just plain crazy! Conflicting emotions tore at her, and she knew it was dangerous to prolong any intimacy whatsoever. His touch made her blood race; his gaze made it hard to breathe.

"Relax, Valerie. We have a lot of work to do." He slid his fingers against her skin as she yanked her hand back. "And we still have things to talk about."

"Then let's get it over with." Trembling inside, she marched down the stairs with all the bravado she could pull together.

Once in the kitchen again, she relaxed a little. While he cracked the crab, she cut French bread and slathered it with garlic butter, then concocted a red cocktail sauce from lemon juice, herbs, catsup and Worcestershire sauce.

They ate outside on a balcony off the kitchen, with a view of the bay. The water was dark under the night sky, but the winking lights of the city glowed like fireflies on the hills sloping down to the bay.

Half lying on a chaise lounge, Valerie sipped wine from a stemmed glass and snacked on crab, salmon and bread. The sounds of the city floated through the air.

Hale propped his shoulder against the railing. "I think we should tell the Stowells we're not sure when we plan to be married, but probably around the first of the year."

"For fiscal reasons?"

He ignored her jab. "We'll tell them that when we get back to San Francisco, you plan to start working for me, as my assistant, to learn as much as you can about the business—just in case anything happens to me. You, of course, will be my sole beneficiary."

"You think he'll believe that?"

"Who cares? It's plausible. That's all that matters."

"What about children?"

"What about them?" he asked, his voice gruff, his eyes growing dark.

"People always ask. Even if you're not married."

"We haven't discussed it. We'll say we're taking one step at a time, that sort of thing."

"Okay." She leaned back, letting the wine slide down her throat, forgetting that this was all just an elaborate deception. With the help of the wine, she pretended that this fantasy of becoming Hale's wife was real. What would she do if she were really Mrs. Hale Donovan? How would her life change? Studying him from beneath the sweep of dark lashes, she smiled. Above his head a slice of silvery moon hung low in the sky, and the leaves from the trees in the tiny front yard rustled in the moist wind from the bay. "I suppose we're going to live here—after we're married?"

"You're the bride—you decide."

"Let's make it easy. We'll stay here. What about the honeymoon—it should be somewhere exotic, don't you think?"

"The Bahamas?"

She shook her head. "How about a couple of weeks on the Riviera and then another week in the Alps?"

"Stowell won't believe I'd take that much time away from business."

Smiling lazily, she said, "Well, I guess you'll have to find a way to convince him. After all, a sophisticated woman with my expensive tastes wouldn't be satisfied with a weekend at the beach."

"You're a working woman remember?"

"But I'm marrying the boss. I expect to be treated like a princess."

"Touché, Ms. Pryce." His gaze, bright with amusement, touched hers. "You're learning quickly."

"Must be because I have such a great teacher."

"Must be."

Hale studied her thoughtfully. Her face, radiant in the moon's silvery glow, was turned up toward him, her smile flashed gently, and though she seemed slightly nervous, she never let up—always kept him guessing. That was what he liked about her best, he decided as he leaned his elbows back against the rail. And liking her was dangerous. He didn't want to feel anything for her—not friendship, not compatibility, not affection. She was just someone who worked for him—someone he had to put up with for six months. Someone who could help him fend off Regina Stowell's attentions while he went about his business.

"Maybe I should call a cab."

He felt a wayward urge to ask her to stay. Though he knew the notion was foolish, he wanted to prolong their time alone together. "I'll drive you." Seeing the protest forming on her lips, he added, "It's no bother, really."

"If you're sure."

"Just let me get my keys."

All too soon they were speeding through the city in his car, the scent of her perfume wafting to him, her leg only inches from his. For the first time he realized just how difficult spending the next two weeks alone with her might be. She had a way of touching his emotions— making him laugh or igniting his temper with one little comment.

At her apartment, he walked her to the front door and wished he could come up with a reason to stay. "I'll see you in the morning—about ten-thirty."

"I'll be ready," she said with a smile that quivered a little as she unlocked the door and hurried inside. "But ready for what?" she wondered aloud as she trudged up the stairs.

Only time would tell.

## Chapter Five

The last thing we need is that cat," Belinda grumbled as Valerie set a rather grumpy Shamus on the floor of her mother's apartment.

Valerie chuckled. "You'll love him. Besides, he'll liven things up around here and keep the rodent population under control."

"We don't have a rodent problem," Belinda said, but reached forward to pet the cat's head. Shamus ducked away from Belinda's hand and hid behind the couch. "Friendly as always, I see."

"He'll calm down," Valerie predicted as Belinda snagged her jacket out of the closet and waved goodbye.

"He'd better," her mother said. She was sitting in her favorite rocker, a beat-up antique she'd owned for as long as Valerie could remember. "So—you're taking off this morning?"

"Yes." Valerie sketched out what she knew of the trip.

"I've been reading up on your fiancée, you know," Anna replied, pointing to a stack of magazines on the table. "He's quite a man."

"Isn't he?" Unable to resist, Valerie picked up a copy of *San Francisco Today*, turned to a dog-eared page and found a glossy black-and-white photo of Hale staring up at her. The article was entitled "The Master Mind behind Donovan Enterprises."

Anna sighed. "All I learned is that the man's a workaholic. It sounds like he spends twenty out of twenty-four hours at the office or wheeling and dealing."

"That's about right," Valerie agreed.

"There's not one word about his family."

"He's a very private person."

"So now he needs a wife?" Anna asked skeptically.

"You know how it is—"

"No, I don't. Why don't you tell me?"

"I know this is kind of sudden."

"Kind of?" her mother repeated, rolling her eyes. "Kind of, she says! I knew your father for ten years before I started dating him. A year later we were engaged and we waited until he'd finished college before we got married."

"Not everyone grows up in the same small town," Valerie retorted, hearing a defensive note creep into her voice and hating it. This lying had to end!

"I just hope this isn't a reaction to Luke," her mother went on. "A rebound thing."

"Hale Donovan is a far cry from Luke Walters."

"I know, but…" Her mother threw up her hands. "As you so succinctly put it, this marriage business is happening so fast I can barely believe it."

"We haven't eloped, have we?"

"Not yet." Anna narrowed her eyes thoughtfully. "But I wouldn't put it past you."

Valerie laughed. "Believe me, that's something you don't have to worry about."

"Don't ship captains have the authority?"

"This is a private yacht, Mom, not an ocean liner. Really, you don't have to worry."

"That's what mothers do best."

"Then worry about yourself. Just try to get better so you can get back on your feet."

"I'm doing my best," Anna replied a little testily.

"I know you are." Valerie squeezed her mother's frail shoulders. "Now, I promise I'll call and write, and the minute I get home I'll race over here with tons of useless souvenirs you won't possibly ever need or want."

Anna Pryce laughed and looked directly into her daughter's eyes. "Just be happy, Val," she said as Valerie walked back to the door. "That's all that matters."

"I will, Mom. *Caio.*" She breezed out of her mother's apartment and tried to shake off the uneasy feeling that this trip with Hale would prove to be anything but happy.

Hale arrived promptly at ten-thirty. She expected to see him in a blue, double-breasted jacket, white slacks and jaunty sailing cap, but was pleased to find him dressed in faded Levi's, an unbleached cotton, cable-knit sweater and leather jacket.

"Casual, aren't we?" she teased as he reached for her large suitcase.

His lips twitched. "I didn't want you to feel underdressed."

"I wouldn't have, believe me." She'd thought about her outfit long and hard and decided upon layering clothes she could peel off if the temperature climbed: khaki slacks, a striped T-shirt, peach sweater and three-quarter-length black denim coat. Not exactly yachting apparel, but simple, practical and comfortable. Besides, Valerie figured, she'd leave the fashion statements to Regina.

He loaded her two suitcases into the Jaguar, and Valerie tossed her coat behind the seat. Hale gunned the engine. With a roar, the powerful car took off through the steep hills of the city and across the bay, to Tiburon.

The morning was clear and bright, the rays from a brilliant sun streaming from the sky to fleck the water and warm the air. Wearing sunglasses and feeling the wind catch in her hair, Valerie felt an exhilaration she hadn't expected. This trip, no matter how it turned out, would be an adventure she wouldn't forget for the rest of her life.

She purloined a glance at Hale and nearly laughed. His face was relaxed and one arm was resting on the open window. His shirtsleeves had been thrust up over his elbows, and his aviator sunglasses covered his eyes. Handsome, confident, a little on the arrogant side, Hale Donovan was a very interesting man and this trip was bound to be memorable. She only hoped it wouldn't end up a fiasco.

They rounded a final turn and drove through tall, wrought-iron gates, which were now wide open. "There's Stowell," he said, his features tensing perceptibly.

A small group of people were clustered on the deck of one of the largest boats moored in the yacht club. William Stowell, a short, rotund man dressed in full yachting regalia, held up his hand when he noticed Hale's car. A slender, gorgeous girl grinned widely and began waving frantically.

"Regina?" Valerie guessed.

"Regina."

"Enthusiastic," she said dryly.

"Very."

Regina was dressed in a fuchsia-colored tube top and white slacks. A broad-brimmed hat covered her head. She flicked one disinterested glance at Valerie before turning all her attention to Hale.

Valerie clamped her back teeth together. This might not go as well as she and Hale had planned. What if Regina didn't know about the engagement? Worse yet, what if she didn't care? With a confidence she didn't feel, Valerie climbed out of the car and helped Hale with her bags. "I assume you brought a change of clothes?" she asked.

"I sent my bags earlier. Come on, it's now or never."

Together, with the eyes of father and daughter Stowell watching, they made their way aboard *The Regina*. The deck, polished teak, gleamed under the sun's warm rays. Built-in lounges and chairs surrounded a table laden with fruit, croissants, champagne and coffee.

William Stowell, a short, puffy-faced man with wiry gray hair surrounding a bald pate, greeted them. "Just in time for breakfast," he said, smiling warmly at Hale and pumping his hand. Spying a deckhand nearby, he said, "Here—let me get someone to take your bags below... Jim, see to Mr. Donovan's bags, would you?"

"They belong to Valerie," Hale said, but handed the bags to the shipmate, anyway.

"Oh, yes, Ms. Pryce..." William Stowell turned warm eyes on Valerie. "I've been reading about you."

"My fiancée," Hale said, making quick introductions.

Regina paled visibly. Her tanned skin whitened, and she blinked rapidly. "Glad to meet you," she said, forcing a trembling smile.

"You, too," Valerie said.

Regina shot a killing glance at her father. "You *knew* Hale was engaged?"

"Just read about it yesterday."

"It would have been nice if you'd said something."

"Hale!"

Valerie turned, squinting against the sun. A tall, stately woman with a cloud of white hair was walking briskly toward them, her arms extended.

Hale clasped both the older woman's hands in his. "How're you, Beth?"

She smothered a smile and proclaimed, "Absolutely wretched! I planned what I thought would be a nice vacation and that damned husband of mine has turned it into a business meeting!"

"You knew it all along," William protested, chuckling. He glanced at Valerie and winked. "She's always grumpy before she's had her first cup of coffee."

"That's ridiculous!"

William's eyes twinkled. "Quit griping and meet Hale's future bride."

"Bride?" Beth's smile wavered a bit, and she turned interested gold-colored eyes on Valerie. "Well, well, well . . . we knew he was bringing a friend, of course, but a fiancée?" Taking Val's hand in hers, she stage-whispered, "It's about time someone hog-tied this one."

"Oh, Mother," Regina moaned.

"Forgive my wife," William said, "she can't let me forget she grew up on a ranch in Montana."

Beth's lips twitched. "After thirty years he's still trying to make a lady out of me."

"And failing miserably," William confided, but Beth didn't seem to notice. She poured a cup of coffee from the service. "Well, William is right about one thing—"

"Only one?" her husband inquired.

Beth ignored him. "I'm not really awake until I've had my second cup. How about you?" She offered the cup to Valerie.

"Thank you." Valerie took a sip and, above the rim, caught Hale's gaze. Amusement danced in his eyes, and he had trouble hiding a smile.

"Let's have some breakfast, then I'll show you to your rooms. Maybe by then Stewart will have deigned to join us." Beth motioned everyone to the small, shaded table on deck.

"Stewart's joining us?" Hale asked.

"So he says, but he's late," Beth replied.

"Again," William agreed. "I swear that boy is always a day late and a dollar short."

"More like a hundred dollars," Regina said coldly, then turned to Valerie. "Wait until you meet my brother, then you'll know what we're all talking about."

"Well, let's change the subject," Beth decreed. "I'm sure Hale's fiancée isn't the least bit interested in our family squabbles."

Hale sat next to Valerie, where they made small talk and brunched on fresh strawberries, flaky croissants and pastries.

Drawing her finely arched brows into a petulant frown, Regina sat across from Valerie and Hale as she poured herself a glass of champagne. "So when's the wedding?" she asked as Valerie pushed her plate aside.

To Valerie's surprise, Hale linked his fingers through hers. "After the first of the year," he said easily.

"Why wait?" Beth asked.

Valerie's throat went dry. "We, uh, thought we should give it a little time. We haven't known each other all that long..."

"So? I knew the minute I set eyes on William that I was going to marry him."

William grinned. "I guess I didn't have a chance."

"Best thing that ever happened to you," Beth insisted.

Valerie had to suppress a giggle.

"Some people like to take their time," Regina said, brightening a little and flashing a beautiful smile in Hale's direction.

"Not like you, though, is it, Donovan?" Stowell muttered. He poured himself a second cup of coffee and added a thin stream of cream. "You seem the type to see what you want and go after it—the way you did with my company."

"Marriage is a little different," Hale responded. Casually he draped his arm over the back of Valerie's chair. His sweater sleeve touched her hair, but she didn't move as he went on, "Marriage is a lifetime commitment."

Regina seemed amused. "Is it? Not according to Stewart!"

Beth sighed and shot Regina a killing look, before explaining, "Our son has had a few...problems...settling down."

"The black sheep of the family," Regina added, obviously enjoying the turn of the conversation as she fingered her long-stemmed glass and sipped champagne.

"He's just a little misguided right now." Beth set down her cup to end the conversation and turned her attention to Valerie. "If you're ready, I'll show you your rooms."

"I'll do it," Regina offered sweetly. Standing, she held on to her hat as a stiff breeze caught the broad brim. "This way."

She motioned with her free hand and led them down a short flight of stairs to the main salon. Though not particularly spacious, the room was well planned. A television, radio, computer and tape deck were mounted in a gleaming bookcase. Lavish built-in settees lined three walls, and a few movable chairs and tables were clustered throughout the room. The cream-colored carpet was thick but durable, and contrasted with the oxblood leather chairs and tucked upholstery. "Through here," Regina said, waving them into a short hallway toward the stern.

She shoved open a small door. "This is your stateroom," she said to Valerie. "Hale is right next door—unless you two would prefer to bunk together."

Hale slid his arm around Valerie's waist. "Maybe—"

"This will be fine," Valerie cut in before Hale could say anything else. Sleeping in the room next to Hale's would be bad enough, but she shuddered to think what would happen if they were housed in the same stateroom. Though she didn't consider herself the least bit prudish, she knew danger when she saw it. And being close to Hale both day and night was bound to spell trouble.

Regina smiled knowingly. "Then I'll see you topside later." Her gaze lingered on Hale for a second before she disappeared.

When Regina was out of earshot, Valerie pulled away from Hale. "I don't think she believes us."

"She would have if you hadn't acted like such a nineteenth-century prig, for crying out loud!"

"I didn't!"

"Oh, no? The way I saw it, you nearly came apart when she suggested we sleep together. You couldn't wait to set her straight." He grabbed her arm, propelled her into her room and slammed the door tightly shut behind him. "Now listen to me, Pryce. You don't have anything to worry about from me. Your precious virtue isn't in any danger. But I expect you to *act* like you want me. We're supposed to be getting married, for God's sake, so don't play up this frightened little virgin act. It won't wash with the Stowells and it doesn't wash with me!"

"I'm not a frightened, little anything! And as for the sleeping arrangements, even people who sleep together sometimes keep separate rooms for appearances' sake!" she fumed.

"Only those with something to hide!"

"Like us?" she asked, eyes narrowing. "Now, are you finished ranting and raving like a lunatic?"

"I was just pointing out your mistake."

"It's not a mistake. I agreed to pretend to be in love with you and enjoy your company, but I don't remember signing anything that stated I should act like some hot-to-trot coed plotting ways to jump into your bed!"

"Just don't play up the ice-maiden bit!"

She drew back her arm and felt her hands curl into fists. "Ice maiden—"

There was a sharp rap on the door. Before she knew what was happening, Hale stepped forward, wrapped his arms around her and ground his lips on hers with such a fury she couldn't speak. Her pulse jumped as he splayed his hands possessively on her back. He shifted then, pressing tight, instinctively molding her against him. The world seemed to spin...

The door to the cabin was prodded open gently, and Beth, blushing to the roots of her snow-white hair, peeked inside. "Oh, I'm sorry—"

Hale snapped his head up, and he grinned wickedly, looking for all the world like a devilish boy caught with his hand in the cookie jar. "Don't be."

"I was just seeing that all your things were in the right rooms—well, you can let me know later."

"No, really, it's all right," Valerie sputtered. Dear Lord, was that her heart slamming against her ribs?

Beth shut the door discreetly behind her.

Hale let her go, and Valerie whirled on him. "What was that all about?"

"I was just undoing some of the damage you caused."

"By mortifying me?" she challenged, ready to do battle.

"By showing my affection, my undying love," he mocked.

"Oh, save it, Donovan!" Dropping onto the edge of her bed and catching sight of her reflection in a mirror over the built-in dresser, she felt totally ashamed. Her eyes were wide and luminous, her cheeks flushed, her lips swollen, her hair falling around her face in loose, unruly curls. She looked wanton and willing and ready. Groaning, she shoved her hair out of her face, then skewered him with an angry glare. "We're alone now, you don't have an audience to play to. You don't have to pretend to be smitten."

"Just remember our contract," he suggested, his expression grave, his skin whiter than it had been.

Raising her chin a fraction, she surveyed him through narrowed, furious eyes. "How could I forget it?"

His jaw worked a second, and he seemed about to lash out at her. Bracing herself, she waited, ready for the next attack, which, thankfully, didn't come. He yanked open the door and strode through, letting it slam behind him.

"Thank God," she whispered, sighing and lying back on her bed. This was worse than she'd ever imagined! His kiss had turned her legs to jelly. Never would she have expected her reaction to be so soul jarring, so violent. Her heart was still hammering out of control!

Slowly she drew in several deep, calming breaths, then propped herself on one elbow and studied her room for the first time. It was compact but comfortable. The raised bed was tucked into the outside wall, and beneath it were three large drawers. There was a small closet near the foot of the bed, a built-in bureau and lamps mounted overhead near the bed and center of the room.

Were the situation different, Valerie knew she would easily be able to enjoy herself here. She stripped off her sweater, found her two bags, placed her clothes in the drawers beneath her bed, then opened a door to what she assumed would be a bathroom. However, as the door swung inward, she realized she was staring into another stateroom—Hale's.

The room was identical to hers, except that the furniture arrangement was reversed.

"Great," she muttered, noting three large suitcases and two trunks propped against the bed. "He must be moving in permanently."

Rather than take a chance on being caught in Hale's room, Valerie hurried back through the door, turned the lock, then spent the next few minutes locating the bathroom and linen closets.

"Find everything?" Beth asked her as she reentered the salon.

"I think so."

"Well, now that you're settled, let me give you the grand tour. William and Hale are already talking business—can you believe it?"

"Oh, yes," Valerie replied. Nothing, but nothing, was more important to Hale than his precious company—or, in this case, Stowell's company.

Beth walked toward the bow, showing her a dining salon, the galley, two more staterooms similar to hers, and the owner's quarters, larger than the others with a double bed, two closets, built-in desks, television set and separate bath. Through another door a small study was tucked against the hull.

"It's beautiful," Valerie said as they climbed to the top deck, where Hale and William were deep in discussion, sipping drinks, laughing and talking. Regina, having changed into a pink bikini, was stretched out on a chaise, sunglasses covering her eyes.

"I hope you're not all waiting on me!" A handsome man, cocky grin steadfastly in place, climbed on board.

"We were about to set sail without you!" Beth snapped, though her eyes grew warm.

This, Valerie guessed, must be Stewart. With coffee-brown hair and tawny eyes, strong, square jaw and deep tan, he grinned warmly as he saw her. "You didn't tell me we were going to have a special guest," he said, ignoring his mother's waspish tone. Shoving his hands into his pockets, he sauntered up to Valerie. "I'm Stewart."

"Valerie Pryce."

"Hale's fiancée," Beth clarified.

"Fiancée? Well, how about that?" Stewart, not the least bit ruffled, slid a glance at his sister. "So someone's managed to tame the wild Donovan beast."

At that moment Valerie felt a proprietary hand slip around her waist. Hale had disengaged himself from

William and was standing behind her, linking his fingers possessively over her abdomen. He made it visible to everyone aboard the yacht that she was his. Through the cotton of her slacks, his fingertips pressed hot and hard against her skin. She could feel their bold impression as if there were no barrier keeping her flesh from his. Her pulse reacted crazily, and it was all she could do to keep her mind on the conversation.

"I guess congratulations are in order!" Stewart said heartily. "Let's toast the bride and groom." With a flourish, he swept a linen napkin from the table, covered the neck of a champagne bottle chilling in the bucket and struggled with the cork. It popped. Frothy bubbles foamed out of the bottle, and Stewart, without missing a beat, poured several glasses.

"Regina...?" Beth asked, and mulishly Regina took a glass.

Stewart held one out to Hale, another to Valerie, then lifted his glass high into the air. "To the future Mrs. Donovan," he said, ignoring his sister's black look. "May she always be happy and as beautiful as she is today."

"Here, here!" William agreed.

"To love," Beth chimed in, her eyes glowing.

Valerie forced a sad smile. She felt a fraud. Already she liked Beth and William Stowell, and she hated lying to them.

"And to a safe trip," William interjected.

They all lifted their glasses to their lips.

Hale tightened his fingers around Valerie's waist. "And a prosperous one," he added.

Valerie's spirits sank to the bottom of the bay. Even in the merriment and celebration of their "engagement,"

Hale's mind was on his deal with William Stowell and the money he would make from it.

Strangely she felt let down. Her disappointment was ludicrous, of course; Hale's mind was always on business—she'd known that from the first time she'd met him. She wasn't going to change him, and she shouldn't even want to. Yet the warm fingers on her waist coupled with a giddy champagne-induced glow caused her heart to beat a little faster. What if? she wondered, leaning back against Hale and feeling the hard wall of his chest against her shoulder blades. What if, during the course of their voyage...Hale's priorities reversed and money wasn't his all-consuming need?

*Impossible!* Or was it?

"More?" Stewart lifted the half-empty bottle from its silver bucket and cocked his head in Valerie's direction.

"I don't think I should," Valerie replied.

"Live a little," Hale suggested, his breath light against her ear. Delicious tingles skittered down her spine.

"My motto exactly," Stewart said, ignoring his father's dark glare. "We may as well enjoy ourselves since we're stuck with one another for the next couple of weeks!" He grabbed the neck of the opened bottle and poured more champagne into Valerie's glass.

The yacht's engines rumbled loudly. "About time," Hale said under his breath.

"Anxious?" she murmured.

"Aren't you?"

Turning, she planted a playful kiss on his cheek and whispered, "The sooner this is over, the better."

"Amen," Hale agreed, his eyes growing dark. He slipped his sunglasses onto his nose and finished his drink, but kept one arm closed around her, and no one on board could miss the implication. Valerie was his. And she was, she realized, bought and paid for like a slab of beef.

Uncomfortable, Valerie slipped away from him and moved to the side of the deck, where she leaned over the rail and watched the smaller boats and the marina disappear. Ahead, the dark waters of the bay beckoned. Sunlight sparkled on the surface, and sloops, their colorful sails billowing with the wind, sailed by.

Sea gulls floated on the breeze as *The Regina* knifed through the bay, turning westward to the open waters of the Pacific Ocean, where she would spend the next two weeks.

Valerie experienced an unfamiliar weakness in her knees. As she watched the harbor recede, she realized that for the next two weeks there was no turning back.

## Chapter Six

To Valerie's surprise, her sea legs didn't fail her. She hadn't been aboard a boat since she was twelve, the summer before her father had died, and she'd expected to experience a little bit of seasickness, but she didn't. In fact, the salt sea air and gentle rumble of the ship's engines agreed with her.

That first afternoon she didn't see Hale for more than fifteen minutes. He and William Stowell locked themselves into Stowell's den and didn't so much as poke their heads on deck. Beth was busy going over meal plans with the cook, so Valerie spent a couple of hours sunbathing not far from Regina. Several times she tried to draw the younger woman into conversation, but was met with only monosyllabic responses.

She sipped iced tea and read until she couldn't stand it any longer. "So," she finally said, closing her mystery novel and looking over at Regina, "where do you live?"

Regina, lying supine on a mattress, didn't so much as blink. "The city."

"An apartment?"

"Umm."

"Where?"

With a sigh, Regina lifted her sunglasses. Her expression bored, she asked, "What's it to you?"

"Nothing—I was just making conversation."

"Okay—well, I live in a two-bedroom condo near the Presidio. I had a roommate, we didn't get along, so she moved out. For the time being, I'm alone."

"Oh."

With a frown, Regina turned onto her stomach, untied the back of her bikini and lay motionless, her oiled body glistening a deep bronze color. "Anything else you want to know? You know, like where I work, if I'm dating, that kind of thing?"

"I guess not," Valerie said, sticking her nose back into the worn paperback she'd found in her cabin. She didn't expect Regina to continue the conversation, but the younger woman slid her sunglasses to the tip of her nose and observed Valerie over the rims. "So what gives?"

"What do you mean?"

"With you and Hale." Regina didn't so much as blink her dark brown eyes.

"We're going to be married."

"Oh, right," Regina said. "But you have separate rooms."

Valerie smiled. "We're not married yet."

"This is the nineties, you know. The 1990s." Regina rubbed some coconut oil onto her shoulder. "It just seems strange that you're not sharing a cabin."

Valerie smiled coolly. "I guess I'm old-fashioned."

"And Hale?" Regina's dark eyes narrowed.

"Deep down he's very conservative."

"Sure he is," Regina replied. "That's why he's considered a rebel in the investment world. The man is known for taking risks—big risks. I don't think 'conservative' is in his vocabulary."

Lifting a shoulder, Valerie turned her attention back to her book and pretended interest in the dogged attempts of detective Matt Connery to solve a murder in Detroit.

"You know, we were expecting Hale to bring along a 'friend.' In fact, I was sure Leigh Carmichael might be joining us."

"Who?"

"You don't know who Leigh Carmichael is?" Regina's teeth flashed in the sun.

"I've never heard of her." But Valerie felt every muscle in her body tighten. There was a studied casualness in Regina's tone—a cool disinterest that contrasted with the gleam in her dark eyes.

"Just how well do you know Hale Donovan?"

Valerie shifted uneasily in her chair. "Hale and I only met a few weeks ago."

"And he never told you about Leigh?"

"Not a word," Valerie admitted, her temper starting to flare.

"Well, at one time she thought she was going to be Mrs. Hale Donovan. I guess she was wrong."

"I guess," Valerie said turning back to her book, as if she couldn't care in the least about Leigh Carmichael or any other woman in Hale's past.

Regina wasn't about to give up. "I heard she was coming back to San Francisco—she's been in Europe all summer—and the rumor was that she intended to settle down with Hale." She twisted on the cap of her tanning oil and readjusted herself on the chaise lounge.

Valerie sighed patiently, but didn't comment.

"I just wish I could see her face when she reads that Hale's going to be married. Unless I miss my guess, she'll cut her trip short and come storming back to San Francisco."

By that time the deception would be over, Valerie thought, feeling an unlikely twinge of sadness. Then it wouldn't matter if Hale and Leigh resumed whatever relationship they'd had.

Though she tried to concentrate on the plot of the mystery, Valerie's thoughts kept straying to Hale and Leigh and Regina. Frowning, she was reading the same paragraph for possibly the twentieth time when Beth stormed onto the deck, poured herself a tall glass of iced tea, plopped onto a deck chair and held the cold glass against her perspiring forehead. "I tell you, that man is a moron!" she said with a sigh.

"What man?" Regina asked, eyeing her mother.

"The chef your father hired! I swear he doesn't know a frappé from a flambé!"

"Do you?" Regina asked, smiling.

"Well, no, not really," her mother admitted. "But it's not my job to know!" She took a long sip from her glass and sank back in the chair. "You know how your father wants his meals."

Regina glanced at Valerie. "On board, dinner isn't a meal, it's an event."

"It would serve him right if I took over the galley," Beth said fervently. "Wouldn't he be surprised if I handed him a leather-tough steak, corn bread and chuck-wagon beans?"

Regina giggled. "You wouldn't."

"Oh, yes, I would. If Hans—can you believe that? A French chef named Hans—gets too uppity, watch out!"

# PLAY THE

## scratch-off game and get as many as

# SIX FREE GIFTS ...

# HOW TO PLAY:

**1.** With a coin, carefully scratch off the silver area at right. Then check your number against the chart below it to find out which gifts you're eligible to receive.

**2.** You'll receive brand-new Silhouette Romance™ novels and possibly other gifts—ABSOLUTELY FREE! Send back this card and we'll promptly send you the free books and gifts you qualify for!

**3.** We're betting you'll want more of these heartwarming romances, so unless you tell us otherwise, every month we'll send you 6 more wonderful novels to read and enjoy. Always delivered right to your home!

**4.** Your satisfaction is guaranteed! You may return any shipment of books and cancel at any time. The Free Books and Gifts remain yours to keep!

# NO COST! NO RISK!
## NO OBLIGATION TO BUY!

# FREE! 20K GOLD ELECTROPLATED CHAIN!

You'll love this 20K gold electroplated chain! The necklace is finely crafted with 160 double-soldered links, and is electroplate finished in genuine 20K gold. It's nearly ⅛" wide, fully 20" long—and has the look and feel of the real thing. "Glamorous" is the perfect word for it, and it can be yours FREE when you play the "LUCKY CARNIVAL WHEEL" scratch-off game!

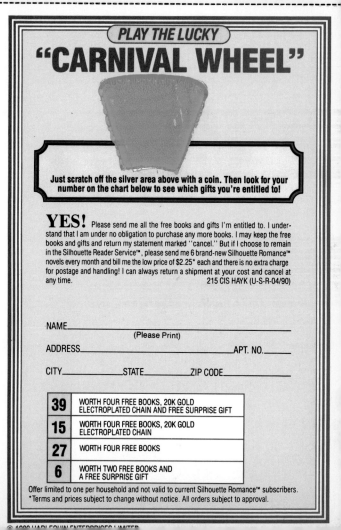

# More Good News For Members Only!

When you join the Silhouette Reader Service™, you'll receive 6 heartwarming romance novels each month delivered to your home. You'll also get additional free gifts from time to time as well as our members-only newsletter. It's your privileged look at upcoming books and profiles of our most popular authors!

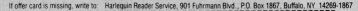

If offer card is missing, write to:  Harlequin Reader Service, 901 Fuhrmann Blvd., P.O. Box 1867, Buffalo, NY  14269-1867

◀ MAIL THIS CARD TODAY! ◀

**BUSINESS REPLY CARD**

First Class  Permit No. 717  Buffalo, NY

Postage will be paid by addressee

SILHOUETTE
READER SERVICE
901 FUHRMANN BLVD
PO BOX 1867
BUFFALO NY 14240-9952

NO POSTAGE
NECESSARY
IF MAILED
IN THE
UNITED STATES

* * *

Three hours later, Valerie changed into a long white skirt and a plum-colored silk blouse. She wore her one pair of diamond earrings and clamped a wide gold chain around her throat. Eyeing her reflection, she touched up her lipstick and caught one side of her hair over her ear. "Good enough," she muttered as a soft knock sounded on the door that separated her room from Hale's.

"Val?" he asked quietly.

Her pulse jumped a little as she quickly flipped the lock. Hale stood on the other side, freshly shaven, his hair combed neatly. He wore a stiff white shirt, crimson tie and black dinner jacket. "You didn't need to lock me out," he said, smiling.

"Maybe I was locking myself in."

"Maybe you're afraid of me." Rubbing his chin, he let his gaze drift slowly down her body, then up again.

Valerie's heart went wild. Pumping crazily, it thundered in her chest. To hide her reaction, she slipped a bracelet over her wrist and laughed. "Don't flatter yourself, Donovan."

"I won't—just as long as you don't kid yourself."

"Wouldn't dream of it," she retorted, but noticed the amusement lingering in his eyes. Arrogant bastard! she thought, ready to engage in verbal battle again but managing somehow to hold her tongue. There wasn't any reason to antagonize him. Yet.

Together they walked through the main salon to the dining area, where fresh flowers and glass-encased candles adorned a linen-clad dining table.

"Oh, there you are!" Beth cried.

Valerie's heart sank. Hale hadn't been kidding when he'd told her the Stowells dressed for dinner. Beth had on a shimmering, floor-length white gown. Emeralds encircled her throat, and her hair was pinned away from her face.

As for Regina, who entered seconds after Hale and Valerie, she was dressed to the teeth in red chiffon that draped over one shoulder and swirled to her knees. Her long hair was swept away from her face and pulled into an elegant French braid. She rained a positively dazzling smile on Valerie, who felt dull in comparison.

*Chin up*, she silently told herself, refusing to feel low class just because her skirt and blouse weren't designer originals.

"Drinks?" William asked, opening a small mirrored bar on the sideboard.

"Just white wine," Valerie replied.

"Manhattan for me," Stewart announced as he swept into the room in a wine-colored dinner jacket and charcoal-gray slacks.

William mixed the drinks, and Beth insisted everyone find his place at the table.

"Right here, honey," Hale said, patting the chair next to his.

Valerie swallowed back a hot retort. Instead she smiled demurely and pretended she didn't in the least feel uncomfortable, though her stomach was in knots and a thin layer of perspiration covered her skin.

"No sign of seasickness?" William asked.

"Not yet," she said. "My father used to take me sailing."

"Did he?" Stewart leaned forward, interested.

"It was a long time ago."

As the chef-cum-waiter ladled bouillabaisse into their bowls from a tureen, William said, "I'm just glad you're used to the sea. Unfortunately we might be in for some bad weather."

"But today was beautiful!" Regina argued.

"I know, but according to the weather service and Coast Guard, there's a storm brewing off the coast of Oregon."

"Great," Regina grumbled.

"Well, no use worrying about it until it breaks," her father said. "Maybe we'll get lucky."

As the dinner progressed, Valerie listened to the conversation and observed the members of this voyage.

Hale was absolutely charming throughout the meal. From the spicy fish stew and crisp salad through dessert, he kept the conversation rolling and even took the time to compliment the chef for the main course—succulent prawns cooked in wine. He seemed oblivious to Regina and Stewart, both of whom watched him throughout the meal. Regina tried her best to be carefree and witty, smiling at Hale's jokes and never once making eye contact with Valerie. On the other hand, Stewart's gaze moved restlessly around the table and he seemed uncomfortable, yanking at his collar, frowning into his drink, his gold eyes wary and suspicious.

Valerie, nervous, picked at her meal. She barely tasted her soup, salad, shrimp or dessert of strawberry mousse.

"Let's have coffee in the main salon," Beth suggested.

"Good idea." William winked at Valerie. "Maybe we could interest Hale and Valerie in a quick game of bridge."

Chuckling, Hale walked with Valerie to the salon. "Don't let these two con you," he warned, his eyes dancing. "They'll play for quarters and by the end of the evening you'll be broke."

"Sounds like the voice of experience talking," she murmured.

"It is."

"Come on, Donovan, you're a gambler," Stewart cut in, his eyes narrowing as he poured himself an after-dinner brandy. "At least, that's what I've heard."

"Not when the cards are stacked against me."

"Only bet on sure things?" Stewart goaded.

"I try." Hale offered Stewart a lazy smile, but his jaw was clenched.

Valerie, to diffuse the tension crackling between the two men, said, "I'd love to play bridge, but I don't know how."

Beth waved away her excuses. "Time you learned."

"I'll be glad to show her how to play," Stewart offered amiably.

"Good idea!" William boomed, already settling in at a small table in the corner. "While Stewart's coaching Valerie, the rest of us can play. Regina, you and I'll take on your mother and Donovan." He settled his eyes on Hale. "How about a small wager?"

One of Hale's brows arched. "How small?"

"A hundred?"

"You're on."

For the next hour Stewart explained the game to her, showing her different hands, bids and cues. Valerie tried to keep her attention on the game, but her gaze wandered often across the room to the table of four. Hale's eyes gleamed. Caught in a fast-paced game, he loosened his tie, unbuttoned his collar and cuffs and rolled his sleeves up over his elbows.

Regina's laugh tinkled through the salon, and Valerie felt a stab of jealousy.

"So, you and Donovan are getting married," Stewart said, shuffling the cards again.

"Umm."

"That'll be the day."

"What?" Valerie turned back to Stewart.

"I said I don't believe it."

Valerie's throat went dry. "Why not?"

"I've heard rumors before."

Just like Regina.

"No woman's ever managed to get him to walk down the aisle." He leaned back and surveyed her through lowered lids. "What makes you think you've changed him?"

"I wouldn't dream of changing him," Valerie purred, goaded nonetheless.

"Then you won't be getting married."

"Only time will tell, won't it?"

Still studying her, Stewart set the cards on the table, then rubbed the back of his neck. "I may as well be honest with you."

"By all means."

"I don't trust Donovan."

"Why not?" Valerie asked, knowing she should defend the man she was to marry and yet unable to muster the right amount of self-righteousness. Unfortunately she didn't trust Hale, either.

"I've heard about him. Some of the takeovers he's attempted have been a little—" he flattened out one hand and tipped it side to side "—unethical."

"I don't think so."

Stewart shrugged one shoulder. "I know, *technically* he stays within the law, but some of his methods are questionable—ethically and morally."

"And no one's ever won a lawsuit against him," Valerie reminded him, inching up her chin.

"Only because of healthy out-of-court settlements." He glanced over to the other table. "Oh, Donovan's careful, all right, but in my opinion he's a little on the shifty side."

"Well, I guess we're *all* entitled to our opinions," she said crisply, surprised at the defensive tone in her voice, "but next time you might keep them to yourself."

"I'm just trying to warn you, that's all."

"Warn me of what?"

"That Donovan might not be completely honest with you."

"Why would you care?" Valerie asked.

"Because you're different from the other women I've seen Donovan with."

"I hope so."

"What I mean is that you're more—now don't be offended—" he glanced down at her white skirt and simple blouse "—but you seem more naive."

"Naive?" she repeated, remembering how Luke had deserted her and how her boss at Liddell had expected sexual favors for her advancement. "I'm afraid you're wrong, Stewart."

"I just don't want you to get hurt."

"By Hale?" she asked, shaking her head. "Don't worry about it."

"All he's interested in is money, you know. Women are a dime a dozen."

"Are they? Well, thanks for the advice, but I know what I'm doing."

"People in love rarely do," Stewart said cynically.

"But I'm not..." She cleared her throat. "Look, it's really none of your business. Hale and I are in love and we're getting married." Before Stewart could guess that she was lying, she stood and leaned across the table. "Thanks for the lessons—and the advice, but, really, I'm a big girl. I know what I'm doing." With a forced smile, she shoved her hair from her eyes and hurried up the stairs to the deck.

This trip was going to be torture. If she wasn't arguing with Hale, then she was defending herself to Regina or Stewart! Fourteen days—and this was just the first! How would she ever survive?

"This is crazy, just plain, downright crazy," she muttered, striding across the deck. Winds from the west had kicked up the sluggish, sultry air. Clouds scudded across the sky. The smell of the sea was tangy and wet as it filled her nostrils. The engines of *The Regina* didn't miss a beat, throbbing evenly, driving the craft northward in the hot August night.

Valerie raked her fingers through her hair and felt the sheen of perspiration on her brow. Between the hot night and the tension in the salon below, she'd begun to perspire.

She heard footsteps on the stairs and glanced over her shoulder to see Hale, his jacket discarded, his shirt unbuttoned, climb topside. "Problems?" Hale asked.

"I just needed some fresh air!"

"It was a little stuffy down below."

She didn't answer, but turned away from the ocean long enough to see him lean his hips against the rail. His gaze held hers for a second before she looked away again, staring out at the ink-black water.

"Stewart can be a real pain," he said slowly.

"So I noticed."

"What happened? Did he come on to you?"

"No." Wrapping her arms around her middle, she contemplated telling him about Stewart's attitude toward him, but decided it didn't matter. Why stir up any more trouble? She just had to get through the next couple of weeks. Then she was out of this mess and out of

Hale's life except as his employee, which was all she'd ever wanted to be.

A nagging voice in the back of her mind accused her of lying to herself, but she didn't listen.

She shrugged dismissively. "I'd had enough bridge lessons for the day."

"And enough of Stewart?"

She chuckled. "He's just worried about me."

Hale snorted. "Is he? I wouldn't bet on it. The only reason he's on this cruise is to try to put a monkey wrench into my deal with Stowell. He's not too thrilled with me buying his father's company."

"So I gathered."

"I guess it's not all that hard to understand," Hale admitted thoughtfully, his gaze touching hers. In the moonlight, shadows from the shifting sea drifted over his face.

Valerie's stomach twisted. Why did he seem so handsome and mysterious? His eyes had darkened to the color of the sea, and the stiff breeze caused a thick thatch of his hair to fall over his eyes in fetching disarray.

"I guess I can't blame him, really," Hale said. "Stewart grew up thinking the investment company would be his someday. Then I came along and tried to ruin everything by convincing Stowell to sell to me."

"So it's a matter of inheritance?"

"Or right of possession. Stewart's worked for his father for years—ever since he graduated from college. He just expected to run the show when William retired. Now, if I get my way, he won't have that chance."

"But even if you bought Stowell out, couldn't Stewart still work for you?"

Hale's teeth flashed in the darkness. "Now there's an interesting thought—Stewart working for me. How do you think that would turn out?"

"Not the best," Valerie admitted, finding the scenario amusing.

"That's an understatement if I ever heard one."

"Stewart doesn't believe we're going to get married."

"He will," Hale predicted. "Besides, it's not him I'm worried about."

"I now, but—oh!"

Hale suddenly grabbed her wrist, spun her against him and lowered his head quickly to cover her mouth with his own. Her lips were parted, and he took advantage of the small space between her teeth to thrust his tongue into her mouth, eagerly moving his lips against hers, twining one hand in the strands of her hair.

Valerie's mind went blank. She pressed her hands to his chest, but didn't push away. Nor did she respond. She just let the kiss happen.

"Valerie...?" Stewart's voice reached her ears, and her heart sank.

Hale lifted his head, and his eyes seemed glazed as they focused on Stewart.

Valerie, too, felt light-headed.

"I didn't mean to interrupt," Stewart muttered, his color rising as he mounted the final steps to the deck.

"It—it's all right," Valerie said quickly. Her voice sounded breathless, and she nervously combed the tangled strands of her hair.

"I just thought I'd say good-night."

"Good night," Hale said. He kept one hand firmly around Valerie's waist.

"See you tomorrow," Valerie added.

"Right." Scowling slightly, Stewart disappeared below the deck.

"Maybe that convinced him we're serious," Hale said, a cocky smile curving his lips as he released her.

"I hope so." Good Lord, why was her voice so low and raspy? Hoping to clear her head as well as her voice, she took in a deep, stinging breath of salt air.

Hale, stepping away from her, shoved his hair from his face. Was it her imagination, or did his hand shake a little? "Didn't you enjoy the show?"

"I don't 'enjoy' deceiving people."

"Well, you'd better get used to it."

"I don't think I can. Ever."

He turned then, his nostrils flaring slightly, and clamped his hands over her shoulders. "Just remember it's for a good cause—your pocketbook."

"And yours!"

He hesitated a second, his eyes luminous with the moonlight. "Especially mine." For a split second his gaze drifted to her already swollen lips.

Valerie was sure he was going to kiss her again. Her breath caught in her throat. Her pulse thundered over the muted hum of the boat's powerful engines. Sweat dampened her skin. But he dropped his hands, turned on his heel and, muttering angrily between clenched teeth, disappeared down the stairs.

She let her breath out in a rush and sagged against the railing. Without exception, Hale Donovan was the most aggravating man she'd ever met in her life! How in the world was she going to pretend to be head over heels in love with him for the remainder of the cruise?

"You can do it, Val," she assured herself, though deep inside she was shaking. "He's just a man—that's all. Just one damned, arrogant, opinionated male!"

And a man, who, with just one kiss, could rock her to her very soul! Somehow she'd have to put a lid on her emotions. She didn't dare let Hale think, even for a split second, that she felt anything for him. If he had a glimmer of how he affected her, the game would be over. Because, like it or not, it wasn't Hale she didn't trust.

With a sinking desperation she realized she couldn't trust herself!

Hale tossed back the last of his brandy. He heard the rain lash at the deck overhead. In the span of three short hours, the weather had turned from calm and muggy to turbulent. The boat, still heading northward, pitched and swayed beneath his feet.

Aside from the crew, everyone on board *The Regina* had retired for the night, but Hale knew that sleep wouldn't come easily. Though negotiations with Stowell were progressing, he felt restless and annoyed.

For the first time since they'd set sail, Hale second-guessed himself. He'd thought that bringing along a woman posing as his fiancée would make things easier, but he'd been wrong. Dead wrong. Fending off Regina's advances would have been child's play compared to dealing with the gamut of unfamiliar emotions that toyed with him.

In less than twenty-four hours, he'd felt everything from elation to jealousy. Worse yet, he'd had trouble keeping his mind on business. Frowning so hard his jaw hurt, he snapped off the lights in the salon and walked down the short hallway to his stateroom.

Once there he yanked off his tie, kicked off his shoes, flopped on the bed and stared at the connecting door between his cabin and hers. Was she asleep, or as restless as he?

God help him, he thought, feeling the boat roll and pitch, but he had to remember that his interest in Valerie Pryce was all just part of their bargain. It didn't matter that she was the most intelligent and innately beautiful woman he'd ever met in his life. And it sure as hell didn't matter that she had the sharpest tongue he'd ever encountered. She was off-limits. Period. And all their touches and smiles, winks and kisses were part of the deal, nothing more.

Valerie Pryce was an actress, and apparently a damned good one, because just for a moment when he'd kissed her, he had thought she'd responded. But that wasn't possible. Or was it?

"Cut it out!" he muttered angrily at himself while squeezing his eyes shut. Soon it would be over. He'd own William Stowell's company and Valerie would leave.

He hadn't forgotten that she had six months to work with him, but he'd already planned to make her life miserable at work, pay her off and be done with her. He couldn't have an ex-fiancée hanging around the office, could he?

A sharp jab of conscience stung him, but he ignored it. Valerie Pryce was a woman, and unfortunately, like most others, money was the only thing she understood. Oh, she could talk about a lot of things—like life and love and happiness—but when push had come to shove, Valerie had shown her true colors. She had a price just like everyone else.

## Chapter Seven

M iserable weather!" Regina grumbled. She snapped off the television and stalked to the window, glaring at the rain beating against the glass.

"It's supposed to break up tomorrow." Beth, sipping from a ceramic mug, thumbed through the latest issue of an interior design magazine.

"Tomorrow?" Regina groaned. "You mean we have another day cooped up in here?"

"You'll survive," Beth predicted.

"I doubt it!"

Valerie, who had spent the day finishing her book, read the last page and tossed the mystery aside. Regina was right. The day had been long. William and Hale had spent every waking minute locked in the den, working out the details of the sale. To Valerie's disappointment, they hadn't even joined the rest of the entourage for lunch.

Frowning, Regina announced, "I may as well get dressed for dinner!"

Beth didn't look up, just flipped through the slick pages of her magazine. "It's still two hours away."

"Well, there's nothing else to do!"

Valerie stood and stretched. She wasn't about to sit around and listen to Regina rant. "If it's okay, I'd like to see the galley."

Beth grinned. "It's okay by me—but remember, the galley is Hans's sacred turf."

"He doesn't like anyone butting in," Regina said.

"I don't blame him," Valerie replied with a cheery smile, "but I think I'll take my chances nonetheless, and I swear I won't 'butt in.'"

"It's your life," Regina muttered, but she offered Valerie the first genuine smile of the day.

The galley, located down a short flight of stairs, was a small, compact room equipped with all the comforts of home compressed into a much smaller space. Several pots simmered on a two-burner stove, and the tangy odor of garlic and onion permeated the air, wafting deliciously.

Hans, a portly man with thin blond hair, meat hooks for hands and a dour expression, was furiously chopping vegetables on the counter while muttering to himself. Diced mushrooms and scallions were already piled in small bowls near a stainless-steel sink.

"Need any help?" Valerie offered, poking her head into the tiny room.

"No!"

"Are you sure?"

"It's a wonder I can cook at all," he grouched, glancing over his shoulder at Valerie, though he didn't turn to face her. "No gas, so few burners, and this room—so hot!"

Valerie thought the galley was a vast improvement over her own pantry-size kitchen in San Francisco. Complete with coffee maker, refrigerator, freezer, microwave, butcher-block counter and stove, *The Regina*'s galley was clean and well equipped. Cupboards and a pantry filled one wall, and overhead, fluorescent bulbs offered bright, if artificial, light.

"What's for dinner tonight?"

"Coq au vin."

"Sounds wonderful."

"If it is, it will be a miracle," he vowed, though the spicy fragrances wafting through the room belied his grumbling.

"You know, I'd really be glad to lend a hand."

Turning at last, he folded his plump arms over his chest. "*You* are a guest."

"That doesn't mean I can't chop vegetables or wash dishes or boil water."

"Did Mrs. Stowell send you down here?" he asked, narrowing his eyes suspiciously.

"Of course not. In fact, she and Regina warned me you wouldn't be too thrilled if I tried to step foot on your 'turf.'"

"Did they?" He laughed heartily. "Well, they were right. Thank you, but no, I can manage very well. There's not enough room for two."

"If you say so."

"But you're welcome to watch."

And watch she did. For the next hour and a half. Surprised at the big man's agility in the kitchen, Valerie found a stool and, like a schoolgirl learning her lessons, observed him adding seasoning and vegetables to his stock, never once taking the time to measure. While the stew simmered, he washed and tore spinach into individual salads, tossed on bits of bacon and water chestnuts and whipped up salad dressing in a blender.

He spoke little, but did take the time to explain what he was concocting. "Now there will be no surprise at dinner," he said when he finally stopped to wipe his hands on his apron.

"That's all right. Believe me, I've had enough surprises in the past few days to last me a lifetime."

He chuckled. "Then perhaps you should get dressed?" Valerie glanced at her watch and cringed. Only fifteen minutes until Hans began serving. After last night's meal, she wasn't too enthused about dining formally. "You're right. Thanks for the lessons."

"Anytime," he said with a lift of one big shoulder.

Valerie hurried to her stateroom, yanked off her clothes, then stared glumly at her closet. If tonight's meal was anything like the previous night's dinner, she again would be underdressed. "Too bad," she mumbled, pulling out a simple black dress and her favorite magenta jacket. The fabric wasn't elegant by any means and the tailored dress was perfect for the office, but definitely too demure for the dinner party. Unfortunately she had no choice.

She wore black stockings and heels, and brushed her hair until it crackled, letting it fall in loose waves around her face. Then, after a touch of lipstick and mascara, she eyed her reflection and sighed.

"Valerie?" Hale's voice called through the connecting door. "You ready?"

"As ready as I'll ever be," she said under her breath. She opened the door and found him as sophisticated and handsome as the night before. Dressed in a gray dinner jacket, black slacks, crisp white shirt and tie, his hair neatly combed, he would fit right in with the dinner crowd. Even if his date didn't.

Valerie forced a smile and cheered herself with the thought that Hale's gaze was warm and friendly as he offered her his arm. Her heart tripped, and for a second she couldn't find her voice. She hooked her hand through the crook of his elbow and smelled the woodsy scent of his after-shave. Dear Lord, he was handsome. She hadn't seen him since breakfast, and in that short time she'd forgotten just how imposing and overwhelming he could be.

The Stowells were already in the dining salon when Valerie and Hale arrived, arms linked. Regina, wearing emerald-colored satin and white pearls, glanced at Valerie's outfit and looked away, compressing her lips to cover a smile.

Stewart wasn't so obvious, yet there was something akin to pity in his eyes when he hoisted his glass and said, "Valerie, lovely as always."

An embarrassing blush crept over Valerie's face. Beside her, Hale stiffened, the muscles in his arm becoming rigid as he helped her into her chair.

William poured drinks and settled into the captain's chair at the head of the table. He winked at Valerie. "Your man here drives a hard bargain."

"Oh, I know," Valerie replied as the salad was served.

"Doesn't miss a trick. I swear, if I didn't know better, I'd think he was trying to wrest this company away from me just so he could sell it to someone else at a higher price."

*I wouldn't put it past him,* Valerie thought, but sipped her wine, instead.

"Now that's an interesting concept," Stewart cut in, waving his fork in his father's direction. "If that's the case, why don't you just cut out the middle man and sell directly to Donovan's buyer?"

"I'm not planning to sell Stowell Investments," Hale said.

Stewart persisted. "You have a history of buying cash-poor companies, turning them around and selling them for a profit."

"Your father's company isn't cash poor."

"No, but still—"

Hale's gaze landed full force on Stewart. "Yes, you're right. I could. *If* I had a buyer and *if* I wasn't personally interested in keeping the investment firm as part of Donovan Enterprises. Once I buy the company from your father I can do anything I damn well please with it."

Tension fairly crackled in the air. Valerie laid a staying hand on Hale's arm, but he didn't notice.

Stewart, rebuked, attacked his salad with a vengeance, while Beth tried to steer the conversation to safer territory. "Let's not talk business," she said. "It's all so boring, and really, I'd think you two would just about be talked out."

"Never," her husband replied, but added, "Miserable weather, isn't it?"

"The worst!" Regina rolled her eyes. "I told you we should have headed south."

"Your father and I wanted to see something different this year," Beth said pointedly, "though I don't know that it matters whether it rains or shines when you're cooped up in a den talking business."

"These things take time," William assured her as the salad plates were whisked away and the main course served.

Beth poured more wine into her glass. "Yes, I'm sure they do, but I know they won't interfere with going ashore when we dock."

"Of course not," William replied, his round face brightening. "After all, this is a vacation."

"Some vacation," Regina grumbled under her breath. "This trip is about as exciting as a case of poison oak."

Beth clamped her mouth shut, and for the rest of the meal conversation lagged.

After dinner they again took coffee in the main salon, but William and Beth retired early. "Have to be on my toes tomorrow, you know," William said with a broad wink as he drained his cup. "I don't want Donovan to pull any fast ones."

Hale shrugged.

"Oh, William, come on," Beth said, wrapping one arm around her husband's. "You and I both know Hale Donovan's as honest as the day is long."

Stewart snorted in disbelief.

Valerie felt Hale bristle, but he held his tongue.

After quick good-nights, Beth dragged William down the hall toward their stateroom.

Stewart poured himself another brandy. "Anyone else?" he asked, his gaze meeting Valerie's in the mirror over the bar. His eyes were friendly, and he lifted his mouth into an inviting smile. "Valerie?"

"No, thanks."

"How about you, Donovan?"

"Not tonight."

"I'll have one later," Regina put in.

"Well, I hate to drink alone, but when pressed..." Stewart grinned widely and shrugged.

Regina closed the bar. "You drink too much."

Stewart raised his brows. "Probably," he agreed amiably.

"Don't you even care?" Regina snapped.

"Do you?"

"No," Regina said. "I guess it doesn't matter to me if you drink yourself to an early grave."

"And does it matter to you that our father intends to sell his business to Donovan here?"

Regina shook her head, then ran her fingers through her lustrous dark mane. "I couldn't care less." She slid a knowing glance in Hale's direction, and a small, secret smile touched the corners of her mouth.

A stab of envy cut through Valerie—not that there was anything about which to be envious, she reminded herself. But that smile, intimating that Regina and Hale shared a private memory, wounded her nonetheless. *You're being childish,* she silently told herself, but she felt a hot stab of jealousy just the same.

"I think I'll turn in, too," Valerie said.

"And ruin the party?" Stewart was astounded. "It's early."

"It's been a long day."

"Correction—a boring day!" Regina said, pouting.

Hale smothered a smile, and taking Valerie's hand in his, said, "Maybe tomorrow'll be better." His gaze held hers for a breathless second, and she saw his pupils dilate suggestively. Her throat closed, and she heard her heartbeat thunder in her ears.

Regina poured herself a drink and cast Valerie a scathing glare. "We can only hope," she said.

"Come on, it's time for bed," Hale whispered loud enough that Stewart and Regina couldn't help but overhear. Tugging on Valerie's hand, he flashed her a positively indecent smile.

Valerie, despite the drumming of her heart, was consumed with an overwhelming urge to slap that crooked grin off his handsome face.

"I can find the way myself," she said evenly.

"I'm sure you can," he taunted.

Fists clenched, Valerie turned on her heel, then marched stiffly out of the room. The nerve of the man! Acting as if all he had to do was say the word and she'd throw herself at his feet and plead with him to make love to her. What ego!

He caught up with her at the door to her stateroom.

"Good night, Hale!"

"Good night, Valerie," he whispered, then took her into his arms and kissed her long and hard, closing his arms around her.

"Hey..." she whispered, drawing back.

He ducked past her into *her* cabin! "What do you think you're doing?" she demanded. "Get out!"

"I will."

"Now!"

"In a minute." To her annoyance, he locked the door behind him and grinned like a Cheshire cat.

"I thought you were leaving."

"I am. Don't worry." He cast her an amused glance. "Do I bother you that much?"

"You bother me a lot."

He smiled crookedly. "Then you must be starting to like me."

"Is that it? And all this time I was sure I loathed you!"

His grin widened. "You didn't loathe me last night."

"Last night?"

"On the deck. Remember?"

How could she forget? "I was acting."

"Like hell."

Feeling cornered, she crossed her arms under her breasts. "I'm a very good actress, Hale. Just ask the producers of *Life's Golden Sands*, or better yet, the actor who played my lover!"

He eyed her thoughtfully and tugged at his tie, loosening the tight knot. "Oh, I don't doubt that you can act," he drawled, "but give me some credit, will you?" Though he didn't move closer, his gaze locked with hers and his smile all but disappeared. His eyes darkened a shade, and he rubbed his chin thoughtfully. "Valerie, I *know* when a woman is pretending and when she's responding. There's something about the glaze in her eyes, the way her knees sag and her weight falls against me that tips it off."

"I'm not going to argue with you," she said, ignoring the accelerated rate of her pulse. "Believe what you want. If you insist on deluding yourself that I'm half in love with you, go right ahead! If it eases your conscience to think that I really would want to marry you, that's your prerogative. But if you're interested in the facts, Mr. Donovan, then believe me, kissing you has no effect on me whatsoever." She was lying through her teeth—what was it about him that made her pride cover her true emotions? And why did she yearn to knock him down a couple of pegs? Pretending interest in her fingernails, she added, "You're just a man, Hale. My employer, nothing more. And by the way, last night—and just now—those kisses? They weren't so great."

"Oh, no?"

"No."

"Then maybe I'd better try to improve."

Chuckling, he kissed her again, and it took all her willpower not to respond to the quick, wet flicks of his tongue, the pressure of his hands on her back, the persuasion of his parted mouth against hers.

When he lifted his head, he quirked one side of his mouth. "Face it, Valerie. You're beginning to fall for me."

She nearly choked. "You have the biggest male ego I've ever seen," she challenged, wishing she didn't feel the telltale flush on her skin. "And I would never, *never* come close to caring for a man like you!"

"And what kind of a man is that?"

"A man who wants gold for his mistress!" she said, unable to hold back the words. "You have a heart of stone. All you care about is money!"

His nostrils flared indignantly, and the cords in his neck stretched tight. He flexed his fingers for several heart-stopping seconds, and she knew instinctively that she'd pushed him too far. Good. He deserved it. She wasn't about to back down.

But his voice when he spoke was amazingly calm. "And you, Ms. Pryce, are a liar."

"Pardon me?"

"Just who's kidding whom here?" he wondered aloud, a small, wicked smile toying with his thin lips. Lightning quick, he snatched her wrist and with a quick tug slammed her body against his. She nearly fell, but he caught her and in the blink of an eye lowered his head and captured her lips with his in a kiss that was as punishing as it was passionate.

She tried to pull back, but he held her close. As his fury gave way to pleasure, he moved his mouth gently over hers and splayed his hands possessively against her back.

No! she thought, forcing herself not to respond. This was her chance to prove he had no effect on her whatsoever. But her traitorous body didn't heed her head. Her breath started coming in shallow bursts, and a wondrous warm sensation swirled deep inside her, heating her in gentle, pulsing waves.

She closed her eyes and pressed her palms against the smooth fabric of his jacket. Gradually she wrapped her fingers around the back of his neck. The feel of the hairs of his nape, the heat of his skin against her fingertips— it seemed as though she couldn't get enough of him.

Hale finally lifted his head, and to Valerie's humiliation, his eyes were as clear as crystal. He hadn't felt a thing! *He* had been acting! "I guess that proves my point," he said.

"Or mine," she responded. Thankfully her voice was as steady as his. Though her fingers shook slightly, she brushed back the unruly strands of her hair and smiled confidently. "Now, I think you know what you can do with all your chauvinistic philosophy on lovemaking. Good night, Mr. Donovan."

With a superior smile, she unlatched the connecting door and held it open, hoping beyond hope that Hale couldn't see her pulse twitching violently in her throat.

"Good night," he said, pausing at the threshold and saying again, "You don't fool me, you know," then slamming the door shut behind him.

A second later she heard the lock slide into place— from his side of the door! As if he expected her to try to get to him! Of all the egotistical, arrogant nerve! Closing her eyes, she let out the breath she'd been holding and wished she could scream or kick or slap the infuriating man. Instead she satisfied herself by kicking off her shoes and muttering a list of oaths a mile long about the particular lack of sensitivity in the male of the species!

# Chapter Eight

Rain continued to pound *The Regina*'s teak deck for nearly three days. Valerie barely saw Hale, and when she did, he seemed distant and brooding. Regina pouted, Stewart grew sullen and even Beth was cranky.

"Some vacation this has turned out to be," Regina growled, eyeing her reflection in the mirrored bar and adjusting the collar of her sweater. She turned her head side to side, and lines formed over her eyebrows. "My tan's fading!" She pulled her mouth together as if it had drawstrings attached to it.

"You'll survive," Stewart predicted.

Valerie, who had read three books, visited Hans before every meal and worked out to an exercise tape each morning, glanced out the window. Streaks of sunlight pierced through thick gray clouds. The sea, though still choppy, was calmer than it had been. "At least the rain's stopped."

"But for how long?" Regina wanted to know. "I've heard that it rains all the time in Oregon!"

"Not all the time," her mother corrected.

Restless, Valerie made her way up to the deck, which, though still damp, was no longer slick with rain. Fresh air misted against her cheeks, and the breeze tangled her hair. The Oregon shoreline was visible. Craggy, fir-laden cliffs jutted upward from an angry storm-ravaged sea.

She heard someone on the stairs, and her breath caught in her throat at the thought that Hale might join her. He hadn't so much as said ten sentences to her since their argument the other night, and she looked forward to the chance to clear the air. Though she hadn't been in the wrong, she hadn't been honest, either. Hale Donovan and his damned kisses affected her as nothing ever had.

"Is it safe?" Stewart asked, smiling as he climbed the stairs and crossed the deck. The wind caught his shirt-tail, and it flapped noisily.

"Safe from what?" she asked. Disappointed that Stewart, not Hale, had decided to join her, she rubbed the chill from her arms and forced a smile she didn't really feel.

"Wind and rain for starters, or worse yet, abject idleness and the chance for boredom to set in."

"I've heard it said that boredom is a state of mind."

"Don't tell Regina."

"I wouldn't."

He stood next to her at the rail, his shoulder touching hers as he squinted toward the shore. For a few minutes he didn't say a word. The silence was companionable, the scent of moist salt air bracing. Valerie relaxed until he asked, "So, how're you and Donovan getting along?"

"As well as can be expected."

"You haven't seen much of him."

"He's been busy."

"So I gathered," Stewart cocked his head and stared at her. "You know, if you were my fiancée..." He let his voice trail off and offered her a shy smile.

"You'd do things differently?" she asked.

"Very differently." He covered her hand with his, pressing her palm into the railing as he linked his fingers between hers.

"How?" Hale asked loudly as he mounted the stairs.

Valerie stiffened. She tried to pull back her hand, but Stewart's grip was firm.

Hale approached. His brow was furrowed, his lips drawn into a tight line as he skewered Stewart with his angry glare. "Tell me, how would *you* do things differently?"

Stewart shrugged, but still claimed her hand. "Well, for starters, I wouldn't ignore her."

Hale turned to Valerie. "Have you been ignored?"

Valerie swallowed hard. She felt cornered. "Not really."

"I didn't think so." Hale glanced at Valerie's hand, her diamond visible through the gap between Stewart's fingers.

Valerie wanted to drop right through the deck, but Stewart seemed to gain strength in the confrontation.

"Give me a break, Donovan. You and Dad have been holed up in that study ever since we set sail! Valerie's had to entertain herself."

"Except when you decided to step in and help out," Hale said slowly, his gaze positively glacial.

"Someone should show her a good time."

"A 'good time'?" Hale fumed.

"Right. Some people take time to enjoy life, Donovan. Whether you know it or not, there's more to being alive than buying and selling stock and preparing financial statements or beefing up annual reports or whatever it is you do.''

The wind rushed over the deck, jangling chains, causing Stewart's shirt to billow, blowing Hale's raven-black hair over his forehead. The cold sea air felt charged with electricity, but not from the storm. ''If I've been neglecting Valerie,'' Hale said calmly, ''I'll make it up to her. Starting today.''

Valerie couldn't stand the tension a moment longer. ''You don't have to do anything—''

''Sure I do. Stewart has a point, doesn't he? We did take this cruise to celebrate our engagement.'' He leaned a hip against the rail, and the dimple in his cheek was visible. ''Besides, most of the business is concluded. Aside for a few loose ends, the deal's done.''

Stewart blanched and dropped his hand to his side. ''What do you mean? He actually sold to you?''

''We'll have the lawyers draw up the papers when we get back to San Francisco.''

''Then there's still time to talk him out of it!''

''I don't think so.''

Shirt flapping behind him, Stewart strode to the stairs and disappeared from sight.

''You didn't have to bait him,'' Valerie accused.

''I didn't.''

''Sure.''

''Look, Valerie, Stewart seems to think I'm out to get him by stealing his father's company. That's not the way it is. I'm offering Stowell a fair price. If he wants to sell to me, it's his business—not Stewart's.''

''Stewart doesn't see it that way.''

''Unfortunately Stewart's a fool. He wants everything for nothing. William would have liked nothing better than to increase his only son's responsibility, preen him for running the investment firm someday, but Stewart wasn't interested in hard work. Nor was Regina.'' Hale studied the mutinous tilt of Valerie's chin. "So now you and Stewart are friends?" he asked, disgusted with the dark turn of his thoughts. But jealousy stung him. He'd noticed Stewart looking at Valerie in the mirror over the bar last night and had seen his hand resting on hers just a few minutes ago.

"Does it bother you?"

"Of course not," he lied, "but, then, I'm not really in love with you, am I?" To his surprise she paled a little. "Because if I were, make no mistake. I'd be mad as hell—and ready to tear him limb from limb. Whether you know it or not, he was coming on to you."

"He was just being friendly."

"Ha!"

"I *know* when a man is 'coming on' to me, Donovan," she said, thinking with a roiling stomach of her experience at Liddell. Her boss had been coming on to her and strong. Shuddering slightly, she said, "Stewart isn't interested in me."

"Do you really believe that? He was all over you!"

"He touched my hand, for God's sake. Big deal!"

"We're supposed to be engaged!"

"I know, I know," she said, exasperation tinging her cheeks pink. "But I told you he didn't buy our story."

"Then we'll just have to try to be more convincing, won't we?" Seeing Stewart touching Valerie, laughing with her, gnawed at him.

"How?"

"Let's start right now!"

Tugging on her hand, he led her back down the stairs to the main salon. Beth and Regina were watching television, but looked up as Hale and Valerie entered. To Valerie's horror, Hale plastered a devilish grin to his face and winked at them before half dragging Valerie into his stateroom.

"You're driving me crazy," he said loud enough to be overheard. "Let's move up the wedding day—or at least the wedding night!"

"What?" she croaked out.

"I just don't know if I can wait!" He kicked the door shut with his heel.

"Have you lost your mind?" she challenged, whirling on him. Eyes bright with fury, she advanced on him.

"Already gone. The day I signed a contract with you!"

He dropped her hand, and she reached for the connecting door, only to find it locked—from her side!

Leaning over a large trunk, he glanced over his shoulder and laughed. "Now you know how it feels!"

"Is that what this is all about—me locking you out?"

"No."

"Then it must be that you enjoy humiliating me."

"Not humiliating you—but paying you back. And, yes—guilty as charged."

"You . . ." She wanted to call him a bastard, but she remembered his reaction before and snapped her mouth shut. "You try another stunt like hauling me in here, and I swear I'll break the contract with you and tell the Stowells everything!"

"You'd lose a lot of money," he reminded her.

"The satisfaction would be worth it!"

A small, amused smile played across his lips, and it was all she could do not to slap him.

She took several deep breaths before saying, "Now if you're done mortifying me for the evening, I'm going to leave."

"Not yet."

"And why not?"

"Because I have something for you."

Oh, no, now what? She watched as he pulled a trunk from the corner, snapped open the locks and threw back the lid.

Valerie gasped as she saw dresses, over a dozen of them, neatly folded away. Green, white, red, blue, every color she could imagine—a veritable rainbow of expensive clothes. "What have you done?"

"I went shopping—well, actually Madge went shopping."

"Madge?"

"My secretary."

"Let me get this straight," Valerie whispered, dumbfounded. "Your secretary went shopping *for me*?"

"Yes, for you. I'm sure as hell not going to wear them!"

"Funny. Very funny."

He chuckled.

"You've had them since the beginning of the trip and you're giving them to me now?"

"If I remember correctly, you weren't in the mood for gifts," he reminded her. "I felt lucky that you wore the ring. Now if you'll go into your room and unlock this damned door, we can put them in your closet."

"You're not serious." Shaking her head, she forced her eyes away from the gowns and back to his face.

Signs of impatience strained his features. "Why not?"

"But I can't accept these—"

"Consider it part of your employee benefit package."

"But—"

"No 'buts,' just go unlock the door. And don't worry about the size, they should all fit."

"How do you know?"

"I checked the labels of your clothes the day before we left San Francisco."

Her anger, still simmering, heated to a rapid boil. "You didn't." But she knew he had. A man like Donovan wouldn't leave anything to chance—not even a simple dress size. She remembered him pawing through her suitcase in her apartment. "You had no right—"

"I had every right. I agreed to pay you to pose as my fiancée, now, come on. There's only a little time before dinner."

"I'm not wearing any of these."

"Don't be so damned proud!"

"I'll stop—the minute you stop being so damned overbearing!"

He laughed then, and a tenderness shone in his eyes. "God, you're stubborn."

She wanted to argue, but she knew that he was right.

"Look, Valerie, maybe this isn't all very proper—at least according to your antiquated code of ethics, but bend a little, will you? We don't exactly have a conventional work arrangement, and I only bought these dresses to save you some embarrassment. I've seen how Regina and Stewart look at you. Beth and William, too. Unless you like their pity—"

"They don't pity me! And as for Regina, she's thrilled that I can't compete with her!"

Hale clucked his tongue and wagged his head. "Oh, you compete all right," he said, leaning back on his heels and staring up at her. "And you know what? She always comes up short."

Valerie's throat thickened. Was he really complimenting her? She searched his face and found his eyes, as gray as a Pacific storm, serious and intense. "Then...uh...I guess I don't need new clothes."

"I want you to have them."

"Why?" she wondered aloud, hating the horrid turn of her thoughts but unable to hold her tongue. "Maybe you're not worried about my embarrassment at all."

"No?"

"Maybe you're the one who's ashamed."

"Of you?"

She stared down at him and got lost in those eyes. "It's just possible you're embarrassed because I haven't molded myself into the image you seem to think you need for a wife—a woman who wears fancy gowns, expensive jewels and has two or three fur coats tucked in her closet!"

Hale sighed. "You haven't embarrassed me yet," he said softly. "And no matter what you may think, I wouldn't judge you by your taste in clothes or the value of your wardrobe."

"Well, that's a relief," she mocked, hoping to break the tension slowly building between them. "I feel *so* much better already. Mr. Anything-for-a-buck does have a set of values that he claims isn't totally controlled by the value of the dollar!"

Hale shook his head, his dark hair gleaming in the soft light of the cabin. "You know, Valerie, you are without a single doubt the most irritating woman I've ever met."

"That must be why you chose me," she tossed back, but could feel her anger fading as quickly as an eagle taking flight.

"Must be," he growled.

Valerie walked through the door to the hall and into her room before she unlocked the connecting door separating their cabins. With a grunt, Hale hauled the trunk into her stateroom and dropped it on her bed. "Wear something special tonight," he suggested.

"Any particular reason?"

He paused at the door and stared at her. "I just want to show you off," he said, then disappeared. The lock clicked softly behind him.

Valerie was left with her heart in her throat. Was he sincere? Or just mocking her again?

"Oh, it doesn't matter," she told herself as she hung up the dresses one by one. Madge, bless her, had exquisite taste. Though Valerie felt more of a fraud than ever, to appease Hale she stepped into a strapless blue dress. With a pinched waist, gauzy skirt and sequined bodice, the dress sparkled and shimmered, billowing softly around her knees, whispering when she walked.

Valerie couldn't help the rush of excitement that coursed through her blood. Of course she knew she was being childish—a new dress, or trunkful of them for that matter, didn't change things. In fact, if she were thinking properly, she'd probably realize that dressing to please Hale was a mistake, one more thread in his web of lies. But she couldn't resist. For just this one night she wanted to play the part of his bride-to-be as if she meant it!

She French-braided her hair, twisting it away from her face, and applied her makeup with more care than usual.

A soft rap sounded on the connecting door, and Valerie glanced up just as it swung open.

Hale poked his head into her room, and his eyes turned the color of quicksilver when he saw her. "Madge has great taste," he murmured.

"Remind me to thank her when we get back."

"I will—believe me." His Adam's apple bobbed, and he stuck two fingers in his collar, as if it were suddenly too tight. "I guess I should've had the trunk delivered to your room on the first night. Would you have accepted the dresses?"

"No—"

"Then I made the right decision."

"You *knew* I'd take them now?"

Chuckling, he shook his head. "Oh, no, Ms. Pryce, I can't begin to imagine how you'll react to the things I do."

"But you thought you could convince me."

"I *hoped*."

She shrugged. "Well, it's only for one night."

"We'll see."

Slightly irritated, she grabbed her clutch purse. "We're already late for dinner."

"Just one more minute." He ducked back into his room and reappeared with a long, slim jeweler's case.

Valerie's heart nearly stopped. *Now what?*

"I think we'd better complete the transition, don't you?"

"Transition?"

"Right. From working girl to—"

"Don't say 'debutante.'"

"I was going to say—"

"And not 'princess.' I can't stand all that stuff."

"From working girl to doted upon fiancée of one of the West Coast's most eligible bachelors."

"That's worse!" she said, but laughed despite herself.

"Oh, relax and enjoy yourself," he chided, opening the case and withdrawing a necklace and bracelet of clear stones.

"Oh, no, Hale, I couldn't—"

"They're crystals, not diamonds," he said quickly.

"Don't tell me—even you have to budget," she teased.

He cocked one dark brow, but didn't say a word, just looped the necklace around her throat, while she adjusted the bracelet. The crystal beads felt as cool as ice against her skin. With hot fingers he brushed her nape, and a small tingle darted up her spine. As for the necklace, the shimmering glass caught in the soft lights and reflected against her skin. She adjusted the strands, then looked into the mirror to find Hale's reflection staring back at her.

The intensity of his gaze seemed to burn through the glass. Valerie's mouth went cotton dry as her gaze touched his for a pulsing second; then she turned quickly away and fumbled for her purse. What was it about him that made her feel as foolishly naive as a schoolgirl? She was a grown woman, for God's sake, and though not worldly-wise, she wasn't as innocent as a child.

"Valerie." Behind her, his voice was a whisper, and he clamped his hands over the bare skin of her upper arms. His breath fanned the skin at the base of her skull, and her skin flushed warm. "I just want you to know—"

Tap. Tap. Tap. "Valerie? You in there? Hans is ready to serve." It was Stewart's voice on the other side of the door.

Startled, Valerie stepped away from Hale, from his intense eyes, warm fingertips and erotic touch.

She opened the door. Stewart was waiting, drink in hand. He took one slow look at her before letting out a long, low whistle. "Look at you," he whispered, nearly awestruck, before he caught sight of Hale.

"We're on our way," Hale growled.

Valerie swallowed a smile. "Be nice, honey," she reprimanded primly, laying a hand on Hale's arm and linking her free hand through Stewart's.

Hale tensed. He narrowed his eyes, but Valerie pretended not to notice as they entered the dining salon.

At the sight of Valerie, Regina's mouth dropped open, but she recovered, motioning to the bar. "Can I get you something?"

"Nothing for me," Valerie replied.

Hale didn't bother responding, but walked to the bar and splashed a healthy shot of scotch into a tumbler. He felt Regina's interested gaze on him, knew his knuckles were white around the glass, but didn't care. His other hand, tucked in the pocket of his slacks, was curled into a fist. The simple fact was that given the least bit of provocation, he'd like to smash that fist into the smug smile glued onto Stewart Stowell's dimpled chin!

Jealousy, hot and venomous, swept through him, and a burning possessiveness of Valerie pounded in his temples. *You're a fool,* he told himself. Jealousy and this overpowering need to possess were the trademarks of a fool—the kind of emotion that he'd always scoffed at.

To his surprise he heard Regina mumble, "Nice dress," to Valerie. The younger woman looked over the expensive fabric, and the mocking glint so often resting in her eyes was missing.

"Thanks." Valerie glanced his way. "It was a gift from Hale."

"It's...gorgeous," Regina admitted, studying the delicate layers.

"Well, come on now, let's eat," Beth said, entering the room in a swirl of peach silk. Her gaze swept the dining salon, landed on Valerie, and she smiled, not saying a word as Hans served scallops in a cream sauce.

Conversation was lighter tonight. The break in the weather seemed to lift everyone's spirits. Stewart laughed and joked and flirted outrageously with her, and Valerie enjoyed his seductive glances and remarks. Hale, the consummate actor, played his part of the jealous husband-to-be to the hilt. He grew even more silent and brooding as the salad, soup, and main course followed one after another.

"So tell me, where did you and Hale meet?" Stewart asked as coffee was served.

Surprised at the question, Valerie, who had talked her way through dinner, was suddenly tongue-tied. She glanced at Hale for help, but was met with a cold stare. The second their gazes touched, she knew he wasn't about to help her out. "I—it was a couple of months ago."

Regina fingered the gold rope at her neck. "But where? At a party? One of those fund-raising benefits?"

"No..." Valerie glanced pleadingly at Hale, but he just sipped his coffee. Apparently he was going to let her hang them both. Well, damn him, two could play at this game.

"What then?"

"Actually, we met when I interviewed for a job at his company."

Regina's mouth rounded into a tiny little "o."

Stewart, who had reached for the bottle of wine, hesitated before taking hold of the neck of the bottle.

And Hale—his cold eyes grew instantly hot.

"Really?" Stewart asked.

"Well, that was just the start, of course," Valerie went blithely on, though she felt Hale touch her leg under the table, warning her not to tread too far. Smiling, she tilted her head to one side and stared innocently at him, though the hand on her leg was positively burning through her skirt. "Since then, well, things have progressed."

"Did you hire her?" Stewart asked, amusement flickering across his face.

Hale forced a lazy smile. "Not until I convinced her to marry me."

William and Beth both chuckled, but Valerie felt as if her throat was welded shut. No sound escaped. The grin Hale sent her was absolutely wicked.

"Well, that's a novel proposal," Regina offered, still thoughtfully rubbing her necklace.

"To say the least."

Stewart poured himself a generous portion of wine, and Valerie realized in that instant that he was a true snob—shocked that Hale would date anyone who worked for him.

As they finished their coffee and conversation dwindled, Valerie felt the strain in the room. Though Beth didn't seem the least concerned, her announcement that she'd applied to work for Hale caused speculative glances from the two younger Stowells.

Excusing herself before she said anything else that might cause further scrutiny on her engagement to Hale, she hurried upstairs to the deck.

A stiff breeze blew from the west. Lavender-shaded water stretched to the horizon to meet a pink-tinged sky. A few thin clouds obscured the lowering sun, and to the north lay a group of small islands, moss green with fir trees.

Bracing her hands on the rail, Valerie studied the ocean and watched a sea gull circle and dip. The first week was nearly over, she thought to herself. All she had to do now was just hang in there. Some of the rigging groaned in the wind, and as always, the throb of the engines hummed in the coming night.

She didn't know Hale had joined her until she noticed a large male hand gripping the rail not an inch from her fingers. Glancing up, she saw the tight line of Hale's jaw, the compressed anger in the white brackets surrounding his mouth. "Why the hell did you spout off about meeting me in an interview?" he growled.

"You could have fielded that question yourself," she reminded him. "But oh, no, you weren't interested, were you?"

"I was interested all right—interested in why my fiancée was throwing herself at another man."

"Me?" She couldn't help but laugh. "Throwing myself at . . . oh, no, you don't think I'm interested in Stewart." She giggled again, and the back of his neck turned scarlet. "That's rich, Hale. Very rich. Stewart and *me*?" Her stomach quivered and laughter bubbled up from her throat.

He yanked roughly at his tie. "Looked that way to me."

"Stewart was flirting, yes, but—"

"And you were leading him on!"

"Never."

"Come on, you enjoyed every minute of it."

"Don't you think you're carrying this jealous-lover bit a little too far?" she asked, shaking her head. "No one's here to overhear you, so you're just wasting your breath!"

"It doesn't matter if someone overhears us or not!" he muttered between clenched teeth.

Dear Lord, he was really playing this to the hilt! If Valerie didn't know better, she'd swear he was actually jealous! Of Stewart! She tried to swallow her laughter, but couldn't. The idea was so preposterous that she giggled again. "For your information, Stewart is *not* my type."

"And who is?"

"What does it matter?"

"Look, we had an agreement," he said, his eyes snapping as he turned and faced her, clamping one hand over her fingers. "And that agreement states that for every single hour of the day *and night*, you play your part. You don't flirt with other men, you dote on me, you act as if the very core of your existence depends on the fact that we're in love."

Valerie's laughter died in her throat. "You're kidding, right?"

"No way!"

"But no one in today's world acts like that."

"My future wife would!"

"Then I'm afraid, Mr. Donovan, you're going to spend the rest of your life a very lonely man. Because no sane woman in this day and age is going to bow and serve and grovel—"

"I don't expect groveling."

"Well, praise the Lord!" she said sarcastically.

"Look, Valerie, we're doing this *my* way."

"Oh, yes, sir!" she snapped. "Wouldn't think of doing it any other way, sir!"

His nostrils flared, his eyes grew dark, and he started for the stairs.

"And by the way, Mr. Donovan, sir," she challenged, reaching the stairs before he did. "You can take all your dresses and jewelry and throw them overboard for all I care, because I won't be wearing them!" Shaking with anger, she reached behind her neck and fumbled with the clasp of her necklace, intending to hurl the damn crystal beads in his face. But one finger caught in her hair and she succeeded in loosening only a couple of pins. A thick curl tumbled freely to her shoulders.

"The dresses stay," he insisted, but his eyes had darkened and his gaze was fastened on the lock of hair hanging against her skin.

"Like hell!"

He swore, muttering under his breath as if he were trying to fight a rising tide of desire. But despite his efforts, he gave in, seeming unable to fight a force stronger than his own will. With one quick movement he encircled her in his arms and yanked her against him so hard, the breath expelled from her lungs in a rush. Valerie gasped just as he lowered his lips to hers with an intensity that caused her knees to turn to liquid. Her heart went wild, her pulse thundered, and she wound her arms around his neck, not because she thought someone was watching, but because she had to steady herself.

His lips were warm and wet and sensual. Closing her eyes, she was lost in the scent of his after-shave, the cool breath of the sea, the lull of the rocking boat. He moved his hands over her bare back and delicately invaded the intimate cavern of her mouth as if he were tasting some delicious, forbidden fruit.

"Oh, Valerie," he whispered, dragging his mouth from hers and running shaking fingers through his wind-tossed hair. "This—this was a mistake."

Heart still quivering, she glanced around, wondering where the audience was. But the deck was empty. She looked into his eyes again and noticed the passion—hot and unbridled—lingering in his gaze.

"Why did you kiss me?" she asked. "No one's here."

He clamped his jaw tight and turned from her, staring instead at *The Regina*'s frothy wake. "I wish I knew," he said so softly the words were nearly lost to her. He jammed his hands into his pockets, and the tails of his jacket flapped in the breeze. "I wish to God I knew!"

## Chapter Nine

We're stopping in Portland," William announced the very next morning.

"What on earth for?" Stewart asked lazily. Flopped on one of the striped chaise lounges on the deck, he winced as he spoke, shading his eyes as if even sunlight were painful.

Valerie, after a horrid night's sleep, was glad for a chance to get off the close quarters of *The Regina*. The tension between herself and Hale was too thick, and she needed a break.

"Astoria's closer," Stewart grumbled.

"I know, I know, but your sister wants to go shopping, and Portland's a larger city."

"And a long way inland."

"The rest of the trip won't change. In fact, we'll be in Victoria when we planned," William replied.

"Whoop-de-do," Stewart muttered.

Beth joined them and scowled affectionately at her son. "Oh, quit whining, Stewart. If you let yourself, you might just enjoy this trip. What's your hurry anyway?"

"Good point," Stewart agreed with a glower. "If Dad's really selling out to Donovan, I don't have a job to race back to, do I?"

Beth wasn't in the mood to pamper her son. "I guess you'll have to find yourself a new one."

At that remark, Stewart lowered the brim of his captain's hat, crossed his arms over his chest and closed his eyes.

Valerie pretended interest in a magazine, though the antics of the Stowells amused her to no end. How a down-to-earth woman like Beth and a stalwart businessman such as William could have raised such spoiled children was beyond her.

As for Hale and William, they were once again holed up in the den, hammering out the smaller details of the buy-out, and Valerie was grateful. She needed time away from Hale. Thinking about last night's kiss had kept her awake all night. What had he meant? Was it possible he was actually falling for her? She couldn't believe it— wouldn't delude herself into thinking for one minute that he cared the least little bit for her.

*The Regina* sailed inland through the mouth of the Columbia River, a huge expanse of gray-green water that divided Oregon from Washington. On either side, forested hills rose from the water, and Valerie was happy at the thought of giving up her sea legs for dry land.

Sunlight washed the hills and glinted on the river. Valerie leaned against a mast and tried not to dwell on the fact that Hale Donovan was the most charming, witty, handsome and downright infuriating man she'd ever met. His humor appealed to her, except, of course, when it was at her expense, and his unconventionality intrigued her. Were the situation different, she decided ruefully, she could fall in love with a man like Donovan. "Good thing it's all a charade," she muttered to herself, scuffing the toe of her sandal against the deck and feeling the wind catch in her hair.

As the captain guided the boat from the Columbia into the deep channel of the Willamette River, Valerie tossed her hair out of her eyes and squinted at the changing shoreline. But as she did, she caught a glimpse of Hale standing not ten feet from her.

He was resting his jean-clad hips on the rail and staring at her from behind his mirrored sunglasses. "'Mornin'," he drawled with a grin.

"Good morning," she replied briskly, self-conscious that he'd been watching her. "How long have you been here?"

"Only a couple of minutes." Slowly rubbing his freshly shaved jaw, he said, "While we're alone, I think we'd better get a few things straight."

*Here it comes—another royal edict,* she thought ungratefully. "Such as?"

"I'm serious about you not flirting with Stewart—"

She started to protest, but he held up his hand to cut her off. "Just for the future, okay? I know I came on like Attila the Hun last night and I shouldn't have, but I just don't want to blow this deal with Stowell."

"I know, I know." She tried to keep her eyes off the thin, seductive line of his lips, but her gaze seemed drawn to his face and his rough-hewn features. "Let's just forget about last night."

*As if I could,* he thought wryly. That kiss had all but twisted his guts inside out. He'd lain awake most of the night filled with a craving he couldn't begin to trust. "That might be easier said than done."

"We don't have much longer."

*And it was sure to be torture—sheer torture.* Just being here with her, seeing her slim, tanned legs move easily beneath the hem of her shorts, watching as the wind tangled and snatched at her hair, observing the tiny span of her waist, was more than he could take. She was getting to him, and his willpower was being slowly eroded day by day, minute by precious minute. Sooner or later something would have to give.

They cruised into Portland under a web of bridges spanning the Willamette. Skyscrapers in brick and mortar, concrete and steel, glass and marble, lined the banks. On the west side, a park, lush, green and resplendent with fountains, stretched along a seawall, beyond which the skyscrapers gave way to sharp, verdant hills. To the east and beyond the city, the spine of the smoky-blue Cascade Mountains provided a rugged horizon.

Valerie couldn't wait to go ashore. After promising to meet Hale and Stewart in a courtyard restaurant, she and Regina disembarked and set out to explore the stores near the waterfront. She mailed a quick postcard to her mother, then followed Regina, who apparently knew the shopping district.

Regina was definitely in her element. They passed through one towering department store to the next. "Well, they're not as elaborate as the stores in San Francisco or L.A.," she said, pausing to sniff a fragrance at a perfume counter, "but some of them are quaint and unusual."

Valerie agreed when Regina discovered a tiny, but wellstocked boutique near Old Town. The store boasted two floors of the most exotic and expensive clothes in Portland. Regina managed to find two hats, three pairs of shoes, a jumpsuit, two pairs of earrings and yet another drop-dead black dress. She handed the salesclerk her charge card, then, as the sale was rung up, turned to Valerie. "This is fabulous," she proclaimed, regenerated. "Aren't you going to try anything on?"

Valerie thought guiltily of her overflowing closet aboard *The Regina*. The last thing she needed, at least for the present, was more clothes. "Not today," she said evasively, helping Regina with her packages.

"Come again," the clerk said, a pleased grin stretching from one side of her pert face to the other.

Regina flashed her a thousand-watt smile and promised, "Next time I'm in town."

Overloaded with packages, they wandered along the seawall, watching sailboats, barges and tugs move upstream against the Willamette's current. Trees shaded the walk, and a dry easterly wind rustled through the leaves.

The restaurant, a narrow brick building with a walled-in courtyard, overlooked the river. Planters filled with colorful petunias, impatiens and ivy were interspersed between the tables. Hale and Stewart were seated at a table shaded by a striped umbrella. They sipped from tall glasses and, surprisingly, seemed congenial.

"Buy out the town?" Stewart asked, eyeing his sister's bags and packages.

"Not yet." Refreshed from the excursion, Regina plopped into a vacant chair and ordered a drink. "But just give me a couple of days!"

"Ah," Stewart joked, "the great American buy-out!"

Valerie chuckled, and even Hale laughed. As a foursome they lunched on crab salads and hot rolls, and for the first time since the cruise began, Valerie felt a camaraderie within the group. Even Hale was on his best behavior, laughing and teasing, winking at Valerie and clasping her hand as if he really did love her.

Later, while Regina and Stewart headed back to the yacht, Hale and Valerie strolled along the waterfront, not touching, but only inches from each other. A jazz band was playing in the park, and they stopped to listen. Couples with children, and lots of single people, were stretched out on blankets in the thick grass, listening to the intricate melodies. The sky turned from blue to amber to a dusky shade of rose.

Hale spread his jacket on the ground, and they sat together, listening, not saying a word, shoulders touching, enjoying the calm summer evening. Slowly, as if by magic, the street lamps lit the ever-darkening night. Skyscrapers became grids of illumination, their squares of light reflected in the Willamette's black depths. Jets of water in fountains sprayed skyward, bathed in the colorful beams of concealed lamps.

Valerie leaned against Hale, resting her head in the crook of his neck. He looped his arm around her shoulders.

"I guess Regina was wrong about the rain in Oregon," she said, staring up at a clear midnight-blue sky. "It doesn't pour all the time."

He chuckled and plucked at a piece of grass as the music continued. "I've been here two or three times a year for the past ten or twelve. I've only seen it rain once."

"So it's just a myth."

"Or I've been lucky." He stared into her eyes for a second, then glanced past the band to the river.

Valerie stared at the column of his throat, so close, so masculine. The shadow of his beard darkened his chin, and the smell of him, musky and male, was ever present.

She tried to ignore his masculinity, but the erratic beat of her heart wouldn't quit and her eyes were drawn to the curve of his neck and the dark hair peeking from beneath his collar. Oh, he was male, all right, very male!

As the music stopped and the band packed their instruments, Hale said, "I guess we'd better go."

"I guess." She stood and brushed the dust from her skirt.

A breeze swept over the water, catching his hair and bringing the heavy scent of the river with it. Valerie rubbed her bare arms, and without asking, Hale dropped his jacket over her shoulders. "You're cold?"

"No—not really." But the warmth of his jacket filled with the scent of him felt natural and right. She glanced up at him and found his face relaxed and thoughtful.

"This has been an . . . interesting day," he said.

"Hasn't it?" *I wish it would never end,* she thought ruefully. Why couldn't this sense of closeness, this tenderness be with them always? Why did they continually go for each other's throats?

They walked to the marina together, and Hale helped her onto *The Regina* as the craft rocked gently. Downstairs, in the main salon, Beth and William were involved in a cutthroat game of cribbage.

"Well, there you are!" Beth said beaming as she won and her husband tossed down his cards in disgust. "You missed dinner, you know."

"I'm sorry—"

Beth waved Valerie's apology aside. "Don't worry about it." Her eyes twinkled. "I'm just glad you two finally spent some time alone together."

Hale squeezed her waist and cast her an adoring glance. Real or fake? True emotions or part of the charade? Valerie couldn't tell. She wound her arm around his

and returned his smile with a radiant grin of her own.
"We did have a good time," she admitted softly.

"Wonderful! William and I spent the day shopping for
supplies and sight-seeing. Then we decided to play some
cards—"

"Which was a big mistake," William cut in, grumbling good-naturedly.

Beth rolled her eyes and continued, "William wants
our next stop to be Victoria. Then on the return trip we'll
cruise through the San Juan Islands to Vancouver, Brit-
ish Columbia, down into Puget Sound to Seattle before
finally returning to San Francisco."

"It sounds like heaven," Valerie said, thinking ahead.
If she could keep her relationship with Hale on an even
keel, and if Regina's good mood continued, the rest of
the journey would be wonderful—if, of course, she didn't
do anything as foolish as let herself fall in love with Hale
Donovan.

"Never," she vowed in a whisper, removing her arm
from Hale's. This trip was just a preliminary test. When
they finally returned to San Francisco, she'd begin her
real job and then she could prove to Hale just how trust-
worthy and efficient and valuable an employee she really
was.

The next three days were the happiest of Valerie's life.
The weather was perfect, Regina charming, Stewart sub-
dued and Hale the most attentive and charming fiancé a
woman could hope for. He stayed at her side, and they
talked for hours about business, world politics, the
economy, sailing, horseback riding and anything else that
came up. The only subject that seemed off-limits was his
past. Never once did he mention his childhood, nor did
he have an anecdote about his teens. Though Valerie

learned a lot about Regina and Stewart, she knew no more of Hale Donovan's childhood than she had on the first day of the cruise.

The following day the wind shifted and with it, everyone's good mood. The air turned breathless and sultry, and tempers flared. Regina was sullen again, her tone with Valerie sharp throughout the day.

Stewart, who had given up drinking before dinner, began mixing martinis again that afternoon. And Hale grew strangely quiet. Valerie felt his gaze on her, but instead of a twinkle in his eyes, she saw something else in those gray depths—something dangerous and brooding. He didn't smile once that day. He drew his brows together, and though he was polite, he never once initiated a conversation.

At dinner Regina was peevish, poking at her poached salmon and complaining bitterly to Hans. "It's not done enough," she said, pronging a flaky piece of lemon-drizzled fish. "If I'd wanted sushi, I would have asked for it!"

There was, of course, nothing wrong with the salmon steak, and Hans, his face bright orange, brought her another piece, at which she wrinkled her nose but mashed all over her plate.

"I'm sick of fish," she said churlishly.

"Well, you'd better get used to it, because it's about all we brought along for this leg of the journey," her mother snapped. She narrowed her eyes on her daughter. "And don't you ever, I repeat *ever*, treat Hans that way again!"

Regina's cheeks burned bright, but she tossed her head and shoved her plate aside.

Beth sighed and seemed about to say something else . . . when William, to diffuse the tense conversation, suggested they go into the salon for coffee and bridge.

Regina pouted and Stewart seemed more interested in the bar than cards, which left Hale and Valerie to take on Beth and William.

They lost the first hand and the next, and Hale barely said a word. Valerie's stomach knotted, but she played as cleverly as she could, considering the fact she'd only had a few lessons. More than once she caught Hale staring at her, his eyes thoughtful, his mouth stern—as if she'd done something to deserve his disapproval.

The game progressed much too slowly for Valerie. She couldn't wait to either escape from Hale's scrutiny or haul him into a private corner and demand to know what was wrong. However, with everyone watching, she held on to her patience and played cards as if her life depended on it.

"We'll dock in Victoria in the morning," William announced. He slapped a card on the table and took the trick.

Valerie was starting to understand bridge, though when William and Beth started their rapid-fire bidding, she was sometimes at a loss and occasionally misplayed.

"How long will we stay there?" Regina asked in a bored tone.

"Just one day and night."

"Good."

"Bored, are we?" Stewart asked.

Regina slid a glance at Hale and sighed. "*We* have important things to do back in the city," she said. "Well, at least one of us does."

"Ouch," Stewart muttered, glowering into his half-full glass of scotch.

"Prickly tonight, aren't they?" William whispered out of the side of his mouth.

Nodding, Beth pursed her lips, laid down a trump card and proceeded to take the remaining tricks, winning the hand.

This was her chance to escape. "That's it for me," Valerie said, stretching. "Maybe someone else would like—"

"I'd love to!" Regina piped up. "Hale, you will be my partner, won't you?"

Valerie was stunned. She'd expected Stewart and Regina *both* to take their turns at the bridge table. All night she'd planned for a little time alone with Hale, intending to find out just what she'd done or said to put him in such a foul mood. But now Regina's eyes were shining, her rosebud lips drawn into an expectant smile.

Hale glanced quickly to William, seemed about to decline, then said, "Of course I will, unless Stewart wants to play."

Stewart rolled his eyes. "I don't feel like being massacred tonight, thank you. Mom and Dad are much too bloodthirsty."

"Then I guess you're stuck with me!" Regina remarked, her dark eyes twinkling as she stared at Hale. She fairly flew across the room to land in Valerie's recently vacated chair.

"Stewart, really, you could play in my place," his father offered.

"With Mom?" Stewart shook his head, but lifted one side of his mouth in a sly grin. "I might misplay a card and she'd ground me—or worse!"

"I *never* grounded you!" Beth responded with an amused laugh. "Not that you didn't deserve it just about every day of your life!"

Valerie left them bickering happily. Pretending she didn't see the furious glint in Hale's eyes, she abandoned him to Regina, who was practically drooling to be his partner. Valerie had hoped that Regina had given up on Hale, as the past few days had been so carefree, but obviously, from Regina's sullenness tonight and the girl's absolute elation with becoming his partner in bridge, Valerie had been wrong. And she'd been wrong about something else—her reaction. Regina's flirting with Hale cut to the quick. A sharp pang of jealousy pierced her. Stupidly she wished she'd never left the table—never given Regina a chance.

"Don't be an idiot," she muttered to herself as she closed the door of her cabin shut behind her. "You don't care about him! You don't!"

She threw herself on her bed, reached for the book she'd put off reading for over two years, only to discover the paperback spy thriller missing. Searching nightstand, table and bookcase, she came up empty. "That's odd," she thought aloud, but wasn't about to go back to the main salon and check again. No doubt Hale was still angry with her, and she had learned that sometimes it was better to avoid him until his black mood passed, which usually wasn't too long.

She heard the tinkle of Regina's laughter and Hale's hearty chuckle. Her heart twisted. "It doesn't matter," she insisted, but as she unzipped her dress, she caught sight of her reflection. Her lips were turned down, and deep creases lined her forehead.

The dress, a pale peach confection provided by the president of Donovan Investments, slid to the floor. Valerie dropped onto the stool near her bureau. Her heart ached. She cupped her chin in one hand and stared at her mirror image. "You've got it bad, girl," she told herself, recognizing the unthinkable.

Bending her head, she pulled the pins from her hair and felt the weight of her braid fall past her shoulders. She unclasped her necklace and dropped it into her open jewelry case. Snapping it shut, she saw the diamond on her hand—that horribly beautiful stone that reminded her that her engagement, this cruise and the attentions of Hale Donovan were all a farce.

Her cheeks grew hot, and she closed her eyes against the truth. Because, whether she liked it or not, she was falling in love with Hale Donovan.

"Dear God," she whispered, the thought striking her like a thunderbolt. She threw on an oversized T-shirt and lay atop the bed, not bothering with the covers. The night was hot, the cabin stuffy. Snapping off the lights, she listened to the noise from the salon. She glanced at the bedside clock every ten minutes. The neon numbers seemed to mock her, and she tossed and turned, waiting for the sound of Hale's footsteps in the hallway, hoping that he might knock on her door. For the first time since their journey had begun, she'd left the bolt on the connecting doors unlatched.

She wanted to talk to him . . . alone. Never before had she been afraid of her feelings, but never before had her feelings betrayed her. *Except with Luke.* Ah, yes, Luke, the reason she'd decided never to fall in love again.

An hour passed before she heard Hale in the hallway outside. His footsteps paused at her door. Her heart went straight to her throat.

But he didn't knock, and she heard him open and shut his cabin door. Straining, she listened as he rustled about in his room and imagined him stripping off his jacket and tie, unbuttoning his shirt, pulling the tails from the waistband of his slacks . . .

Clamping her teeth together and clenching her fists around the thin blanket covering her bed, she willed herself to stay in her room, because if she made the first move, opened the door that was not only a physical barrier but the symbol of all that was between them, what would he say? What would she do? How could she stop herself from fulfilling the erotic fantasy of falling into bed with him?

She heard him sigh, and her heart stirred. Squeezing her eyes shut, she tried to sleep, only to stare at the clock and watch the minutes slip slowly by.

"Sleep—sleep," she told herself.

She must have dozed, because the next time she looked at the clock the neon numbers flashed two-thirty. The cabin was hot and stuffy, her skin damp with sweat.

With a groan, she tossed back the sheet she must have pulled over her and sat up, feet dangling from the bed. She glanced at the connecting door, and her pulse leaped. She loved him. It was that simple.

Angry with herself, she shoved her hair out of her eyes. How could she have fallen for a man like Hale Donovan, a man who valued a dollar more than anything, a man who seemed to have no past, a man willing to hire a woman to pretend to be his fiancée in order to deceive a friend and businessman?

Her head began to throb. *And are you any better? William and Beth Stowell have done nothing but kind things for you and yet you continue to lie to them—go along with this cheap facade.*

Knowing that sleep was impossible, she found her slippers and made her way through the darkened craft to the deck. She needed fresh air and space and time to think.

Once on deck she felt better. Moonlight cast a silvery path on the dark water, and stars blinked back at themselves on the inky surface. There wasn't a breath of wind, and the ship, aside from the churning engines, was still and quiet.

Taking several deep breaths, Valerie walked to the side of the boat and rested her elbows on the rail, staring into the black water.

Sweat collected on her forehead. She closed her eyes for a second and experienced the uncanny sensation that someone was watching her every move. The hairs on the back of her neck bristled.

"What's the matter—couldn't sleep?" Hale's voice cut through the stillness.

Valerie nearly jumped out of her skin. As she whirled, she caught sight of him, stripped naked to his waist, the muscles of his chest and arms visible in the half-light. Her eyes were drawn to the dark mat of hair covering hard pectoral muscles and the washboard of his abdomen. "I—I didn't know you were here."

He didn't answer her, just regarded her with wary eyes.

"But I'm glad you are," she forged on.

"Are you?"

What was this new game he was playing?

"Why?"

"I thought we needed to talk."

He lifted a dark brow, and hooking his thumbs into the belt loops of his jeans said, "So talk."

"Something's wrong."

"What?"

"That's what I'd like to know. Ever since you came up on deck this morning, you've been moody."

"Have I?"

He was baiting her. She knew it. Yet she couldn't help but rise like a trout striking at a fisherman's lure. "Haven't you?"

He lifted one shoulder; the muscles flexed for a brief second. Valerie's chest tightened.

"What is it, Hale? What's wrong?"

His eyes darkened. He stared at her and said, "You lied to me."

The accusation hung suspended between them. What was he talking about? "Lied?" Shaking her head, she turned one hand palm up. "I never lied about any—"

"No?" he cut in angrily, his lips twisting into a sardonic grin.

"No."

"You're sure?"

"Positive!"

"Then tell me," he said slowly, his nostrils flaring. "Who's Luke?"

## Chapter Ten

How do you know about Luke?" she asked, shaken.

"This…" He tossed a paperback book into the air and caught it deftly. Even in the darkness she recognized the cover of the novel she'd misplaced earlier in the evening.

"Where'd you get that?"

"You left it in the salon. I picked it up to give it to you, and it fell open to the first page."

He didn't have to say another word. Luke had given her the book two years before. She knew the inscription by heart. "For now and always—my heart will remain in your hands. I love you, Luke." It had been an anniversary gift—given her on the one year anniversary of the day she'd met Luke in her political science class. He'd left her one week after giving her the book.

Striding across the deck, he handed her the paperback. "I thought there wasn't anyone else."

"There isn't."

"So why bring the book with you? As a reminder?"

"No..." She flipped through the pages, then tossed the paperback onto a nearby table. With a frown she admitted, "it's taken this long to get over him."

In the shadowy moonlight, Hale's face appeared rugged, his anger clear in his angular features. "How long?"

"Two years."

"And there's no chance of the two of you getting back together?"

"No!" she snapped, then bit her tongue and tried vainly to control her rapidly escalating temper. "And what business is it of yours anyway?"

"I just don't want him showing up and becoming the fly in the ointment, so to speak. You said there were no boyfriends or jealous lovers that I'd have to worry about."

"There aren't."

"Except for Luke."

"Except for Luke," she repeated, goaded and wishing to knock Hale down a couple of pegs. He had no right to make her feel guilty about loving someone before she'd met him and she intended to let him know it. "Nowhere in our agreement did it say I wasn't allowed to have a past. What happened two years ago can't possibly matter."

"Maybe."

She couldn't stop herself. His high-handedness brought out the worst in her. Shaking, she pushed herself upright and tilted her face upward, her eyes blazing into his. "Well, at least I *have* a past. I have friends and family and yearbooks and memories of my life for the past twenty-four years, but you—" she gestured wildly with her hands "—as far as I know, you didn't exist until you entered college. You have nothing, not one single thing to prove you were even alive!"

Sucking in a swift breath, he surrounded both her wrists with steel-strong fingers. "Enough!"

"What is it, Hale? What are you hiding?"

"Nothing, damn it!"

"Well, neither am I!" She yanked her hands back and started for the stairs, but he caught up with her.

As quick as a cat, he caught one hand in his and whipped her around. "What happened to our truce?"

"You abused it—by prying!" She held up the paperback and wagged it in his face.

"And you abused it by lying."

"I never lied."

"Just left out some important details."

"But not my whole life, Hale," she said, letting out her breath. "I didn't hide my whole damned life from you. You met my mother, saw where I lived, asked questions and I answered. But me, I'm faced with a brick wall."

"Maybe I don't have a past," he said softly.

"That's crazy—"

"It's very sane. Believe me." He relaxed his grip, but kept his fingers around her wrist. In the half-light she noticed a sadness steal across his features, gentling the hard angles of his face.

What had he been like as a boy? she wondered, and ached inside that she hadn't known him then. Had he always been so jaded, so callous—or had his past shaped him into the hard-edged businessman he'd become?

He lowered his eyes to her lips and swallowed. Gently he moved his fingertips along the insides of her wrist. Slowly he tugged, pulling her forward, bending his head and suspending his mouth above hers, his breath fanning her chin. "Oh, Valerie," he murmured on a sigh as soft as the night. "Sweet, Valerie..." He touched his lips to hers, tasting and feeling.

Valerie's pulse leaped to life as his kiss, starting so chaste, deepened with a passion that flowed from his body to hers. Her heart clamored. She pressed her body to his, her soft flesh molding perfectly against his thighs, hips and chest.

Taking her hands within his, he surrounded her, wrapping his arms so tightly around her that her breasts were thrust against him. Covered only by the thin T-shirt, her nipples were pressed intimately against his rock-hard chest. Responding to the nearness of him, smelling the musky scent of his maleness, tasting the salt on his lips, she pressed closer, opening her mouth, feeling her nipples harden and ache. *Love me,* she silently begged.

"What am I going to do with you?" he murmured into her open mouth. His tongue penetrated her mouth just then, causing a quicksilver flame to shoot through her blood, stirring a response so deep within her she quivered to her very soul.

Pulling her wrists free, she wrapped her arms willingly around his neck and returned his kisses with the fire of her own. What was there about this complex man that brought her close to tears one second, fired her with fury the next, then within a split second consumed her with a longing so intense she could only think of making love to him?

She was warm inside—with need and want. Warm with secret fires that no other man had ever stoked. *Please, Hale, love me,* her mind screamed silently, while she battled that very love herself.

He lifted his head, his eyes silver with passion, his hands shaking as he placed them on each side of her face. "This—this can't happen," he rasped, trying and failing to control his breathing. "Not yet."

"Not ever," she agreed.

"Oh, God." He ground his teeth and released her, clearing his throat and shoving his hair from his face. "I should never have hired you. I should've known the first time I laid eyes on you that this would be a mistake!" *But instead I persisted—hounding you—nearly forcing you because deep inside I wanted this moment, I wanted to feel you tremble in my arms. Damn it, from the first moment I saw you, I wanted to make love to you.*

Hale walked backward until his buttocks thumped against a mast. His blood thundered, his head pounded and his heart was thudding like a sledgehammer. Mouth dry, he slammed his eyes shut against the seductive vision she created. With moonlight in her hair, her eyes glazed with desire, he could barely control himself. He clenched his fists behind his back and pressed the back of his hands hard against the mast. "I think we'd better call it a night, Valerie."

Before he did anything foolish like kissing her again, he forced his eyes open and strode to the stairs. His steps were lightning quick as he headed straight to the cabin. Damn, but his hands were shaking and the fire in his loins wouldn't quit. Just the thought of her, warm and pliant in his arms, was enough to turn him inside out.

He threw himself on the hard bed. Then moaning, he rolled over and squeezed his eyelids shut, knowing he'd never fall asleep and trying to block out all thoughts of her.

But he heard her on the stairs, shuddered as her door clicked open and closed again, and wished to God he'd never set eyes on her!

*The Regina* plowed through the Strait of Juan de Fuca to moor in Victoria the next morning. Valerie told herself to forget the past night, but the moment she saw

Hale, she knew their meeting the night before wouldn't soon be forgotten. His gaze shifted away from hers, and the corners of his mouth were pulled downward.

Valerie pretended interest in the view, but she knew the instant his gaze returned with a sizzling intensity that cut her to the bone. Her fingers whitened around the railing, but she kept her gaze glued to the sea as *The Regina* slowed in the harbor.

Sailboats, cabin cruisers and every other boat imaginable vied for position in the marina. Tall masts and rigging swayed in the breeze, and the boats rocked with the lapping water. White hulls sparkled in the morning light.

Beyond the array of vessels, the waterfront of Victoria, a walkway and street were bustling with morning activity. Already tourists strolled near the water, and cars and buses buzzed past. Beyond the street, Valerie saw a wide expanse of manicured lawn and shrubbery in full bloom—the grounds of a copper-domed Parliament building that looked like a cross between an English castle and a Muslim mosque. High overhead, while birds—probably pigeons and sea gulls circled against a flawless blue sky, a red-and-white Canadian flag snapped in the wind.

"This is one of my favorite cities," Beth proclaimed as she joined Hale and Valerie on deck. "So much culture! So much life!" With a smile, she stared at the view and tucked a few strands of white hair under a wide-brimmed hat, then pushed a pair of sunglasses onto her nose. "I can't wait to go shopping. All those interesting shops and English pubs. And high tea—be sure to take high tea."

"Oh, we will," Hale agreed easily, to Valerie's surprise. After last night, she'd expected him to keep his distance. "As a matter of fact, we'll take breakfast ashore."

"What a marvelous idea! I think we will, too. I'll give Hans the word not to bother this morning." She disappeared down the stairs, leaving Hale and Valerie alone.

"Come on," Hale suggested, grabbing her hand, "let's leave now, before we get stuck with Regina and Stewart again."

Valerie linked her fingers with his and cocked her head to glance up at him. "Are you sure this is a good idea?"

"No, as a matter of fact it's probably one of the worst I've had in a while."

"Worse than a phony engagement?"

He groaned. "Even I'm beginning to regret that!" But his eyes crinkled at the corners, and he whispered, "It's working, isn't it?"

"You tell me."

He squeezed her hand. "Too well, I'm afraid." Together they strolled along the docks, then wended their way through the narrow streets, where horse-drawn carriages competed with cars and trucks. Bookstores, china shops, art galleries and authentic English pubs were clustered together in brick squares where baskets of flowers hung from old-fashioned lampposts.

Hale and Valerie ate Belgian waffles and cheese blintzes in a tiny café overlooking the square. He didn't mention their chance moonlight meeting on the deck, and neither did she, though when she caught him staring at her over the rim of his cup, his eyes were penetrating and dark.

*He's trying to pretend last night didn't exist, too,* she realized. *But it will always be there.*

Her stomach began to churn, and she shoved the remains of her breakfast aside. Twirling the cup nervously in her hands, she said, "What do you want to see next?"

"It doesn't matter."

"The gardens? Museum? Shops?"

"You choose," he suggested, then grabbed one of her hands with his own. "But first, tell me about Luke."

"There's nothing to tell."

He didn't believe her. His eyes as much as called her a liar. "There must have been something."

"Once, maybe," she said with a shrug. Withdrawing her hand, she cradled her coffee and settled back in her chair. "I met him in college. He was brilliant, but more into surfing than school. He didn't have to work at studying much. The first year we were together everything was fine, but after that..." She stared into her cup, as if she could find some answers to questions that had flitted through her mind for two years. "He decided he had to find himself. So he gave up everything—a scholarship to grad school, his Porsche, his surfboard and me to trek around Montana."

"What's in Montana?"

"I wish I knew. Or maybe I don't."

"Another woman?"

She swallowed against a knot in her throat. "I don't know," she admitted, sipping from her now-cold cup. "He was pretty vague. He knew some guy who had a cabin in the mountains and he thought he'd spend the summer there. That was two years ago, and I haven't heard from him since."

"You loved him?"

She'd asked herself that same question a thousand times. "I thought I did."

"And now?"

"Now I've convinced myself it couldn't have been love. Otherwise it wouldn't have ended."

Hale's lips twitched. "You—a romantic? I never would have guessed. I thought you were a pragmatist."

"I am . . . usually."

"But you think real love endures forever."

"Don't you?"

She expected him to say that real love didn't exist. Instead he frowned. "I don't know." His gaze touched hers for a magical split second. "I just don't know."

The waiter came with the check, and as they left, Valerie linked her arm through his and pushed all thoughts of Luke and their dead-end relationship aside. No, she'd never really loved Luke, and now it didn't matter. Luke was part of her past. Hale, she hoped, was her future.

Hale insisted upon a carriage ride, signaling a driver in a black top hat and paying the fare. They climbed into the back of the open spring buggy, and at the crack of a whip, the horse, a heavy-haunched gray gelding, clopped noisily slowly down the street.

Slinging his arm around Valerie's shoulders, Hale held her close as the driver-cum-tour guide pointed out spots of interest. The sky was vibrant and blue, the air filled with the scent of blossoms, sea and horse. Feeling the romance of their adventure together, Valerie sighed contentedly and snuggled close to Hale.

"Happy?" he asked, stroking her hair.

"Mmm."

She could hear the steady beat of his heart over the sharp click of metal horseshoes as they rode into Chinatown through an ornate gate guarded by two hand-carved lions.

Nestled in Hale's arms, Valerie watched the bustle of the city and wished the day would never end.

They had high tea in the Crystal Garden, a glass-encased structure that was alive with lush indoor gardens. The building smelled of rich soil and exotic plants, and the sound of birds twittering reverberated against the panes.

Valerie and Hale sat at a small table, sipped tea and munched on finger sandwiches. Hale was charming and relaxed, his gray eyes warm, his smile contagious.

"Beth was right, this is a beautiful city," Valerie finally said as conversation waned.

"Maybe we should spend the night."

She nearly choked on a swallow of tea. "Here—together?"

He glanced around the room at the glossy vines and trees. "Not here—I thought you'd prefer a quaint Victorian inn."

"I think we'd better stay on the yacht."

"In separate cabins?"

She raised her chin an inch. "What are you suggesting?" Though she tried to sound indignant, her voice betrayed her and she could feel her eyes sparkling.

Setting his cup down, he stared straight into her eyes. "We've ignored what happened last night long enough, don't you think?"

"I thought you wanted to forget about it."

"I tried. It's impossible."

She couldn't argue that point. She sipped from her cup again and discovered that her hands were shaking. "I'm not interested in an affair," she said bluntly, her cheeks burning. "I told you that at the beginning."

"I know, Valerie," he said softly. "And I wasn't, either. At least, I didn't think so. But you've made me change my mind."

She shoved back her chair, its legs scraping on the floor. "I think we'd better go—"

He caught her wrist. "You can deny it all you want, you know, but there's something between us—something more than friendship."

"I don't think we're friends."

"But we could be lovers."

Dear God, was that her heart pounding so loudly? "What we are is business associates. Nothing more."

"You're kidding yourself."

"I don't think so." Rather than continue the argument, which was quickly escalating into one of their volatile battles, Valerie strode outside and started walking toward the marina.

Hale caught up with her, matching her furious strides with his own. "Don't try to make me believe you don't know what's happening," he said, "because you felt it, too."

A lie formed on her tongue, but he shook his head, holding one finger to her lips and shushing her as they walked.

"And don't expect me to believe that you were only acting last night. We were alone and you responded, and whether you want to believe it or not, Valerie—" he took one long stride and planted himself in front of her "—we're falling in love!"

*Love?* She stopped short. Was he serious? *Love?* "I think you're confusing love with lust."

"Not me. I know both."

"Do you? And who were you in love with? Leigh what's-her-name?"

He laughed then, throwing back his head at the thought. "No, not Leigh. And her name's Carmichael. She'd be devastated that you didn't know who she was."

"Sorry—" She tried to brush past him, but he caught her shoulders, holding her squarely in front of him on the sidewalk while other pedestrians had to file around them. "This looks ridiculous," she ground out.

"Leigh never meant anything to me."

"She was your lover."

Hale sighed. "That was a long time ago."

"Not according to Regina."

"Since when do you believe her?" he asked, his eyes twinkling with amusement. "Don't worry about Leigh. She's out of my life. Come on." As if the conversation had ever existed, as if they'd never said one cross word, he grabbed her hand, dashed across the street and started walking.

"Where are we going?"

"To an authentic English pub."

"We just ate."

He flashed her his lazy grin. "I know, but we've only got so much time and I'd like to take you on in a game of darts."

"Darts?" *Was he out of his mind?* But she didn't argue, and after wandering through a couple of antique stores and a candy shop, he guided her to a small, dark pub where they served fish-and-chips, kidney pie and dark ale.

Valerie relaxed, ate as much batter-dipped cod as she could stand, then surprised Hale by beating him once at darts. In the next two games, she lost.

By the time they headed back to *The Regina*, the sky was dark, the air cool. Lights blazed in the surrounding buildings as they walked along the waterfront.

Hale draped his arm around her shoulder, and she didn't object. This day had been too perfect, she didn't want to spoil it, and his hand on her arm, so possessive and warm, felt right.

Moonlight ribboned across the dark water near the marina and the sea breeze lifted Valerie's hair. She glanced at Hale, and her heart tripped at the sight of his strong profile. Dear Lord, how she loved him. She'd known him less than two weeks, and he was the one man with whom she couldn't fall in love. Nonetheless she had. Despite all her vows and self-made promises, she'd fallen for him.

Inside, the boat was still and quiet—and warm from the hot summer's day. The Stowells weren't yet aboard, and apparently the captain and crew had gone ashore to sample the nightlife. She and Hale were alone. Completely alone on the gently rocking boat. They both knew it, though neither mentioned the obvious.

"It's late," she said.

"What about a nightcap?"

"I don't think so." The last thing she needed was a drink! Staring into Hale's erotic gray eyes, seeing the taut angle of his jaw, the sheen of perspiration on his skin, the cords of his neck, the muscles of his back moving fluidly as he strode about the salon, she decided she had to be careful. "I'd better say good-night."

"We don't have to, you know."

"Of course we do."

"This could go on and on forever."

He was so close, his breath fanned her face. The heat from his body radiated to hers. "I don't think so."

"Always the proper lady, eh?" With one finger he traced the curve of her jaw, then inched up her chin to touch her lips.

"Proper? No. A lady? Sometimes. But I try my best to be a smart woman." Valerie's insides quivered, but she forced herself to stand perfectly still. She couldn't let him know what a powerful effect he had on her—already he guessed how she felt.

His finger trailed down her neck to rest at the tiny circle of bones at her throat. He outlined them slowly, watching in fascination the trembling pulse encased within. "Let go, Valerie," he suggested, wrapping his strong arms around her. "For once in your life, trust your instincts."

Lowering his head, he brushed his lips slowly over hers. Her blood caught fire, heating her from the inside out as his lips grew harder, more insistent.

She tried to fight the overpowering urge to surrender, but her eyes closed and she leaned against him, opening her lips to the sweet, wet embrace of his tongue, feeling his hands tangle in her hair.

Her head lolled back, and she moaned as Hale kissed the curve of her throat, and lower as he trailed his tongue against her skin to skim the neckline of her dress and ignite fires of desire on the skin beneath.

Her breasts ached, and willful thoughts invaded her mind. *What would it hurt? He said he loved you didn't he? Believe him—trust him. For once in your life, Valerie, take some happiness.*

When he lifted her off of her feet, she didn't protest, but clung to him, her hair spilling over his arm, her eyes watching his face beneath lowered lids. He kissed her at the door to their cabins, and she returned his kiss with ardor, running her fingers over the coarse hair at his nape.

She closed her ears to the nagging doubts crowding her mind, thought only of the feel of his lips and hands, the warmth seeping through her.

"Will you stay with me?" he murmured against her ear, and his very breath fanned the flames of already-rampant desire.

She could barely breathe as he kissed her and carried her into his cabin. Somewhere in the back of her mind she knew she was making an irrevocable mistake, but she couldn't stop returning his kisses. She loved him. And that was all that mattered.

He splayed his hands across her back, and the smell of him was everywhere as he laid her across the bed, falling gently over her and stroking her rib cage with the flat of his hand.

"Valerie, sweet, sweet Valerie," he rasped, his breath short and swift. Placing one hand between her breasts, he felt the pounding of her heart. "Let me love you."

He moved his hand then, cupping a breast through the soft cotton fabric. Her nipple hardened, and she sucked in a swift breath, realizing just what was happening. The heat swelling deep inside was burning with a want she knew only he could fill.

He moved, stroking her breast before she gasped for quick gulps of air and rolled away. "N-no," she cried, choking on the horrid word. Her body begged for more of his sweet, gentle touch, but she forced herself to think beyond this one glorious night.

"I love you."

Weakening, she saw desire burning bright in his eyes and knew that lust was talking. "P-please, don't—"

"Marry me, Valerie."

*Marriage?* "Don't say... You don't have to—"

"This isn't an obligation!" he ground out, his teeth flashing in the darkness as she scrambled to her feet.

Anger and confusion clouded his eyes, and she remembered the last time she'd been in this position, when her boss at Liddell had forced his hard, heaving body on hers and begged her to let him make love to her. Fortunately she'd escaped—and she'd wanted to. But this was worse. She longed to stay with him—her body screamed to join with his.

Stupidly she reached forward, touching the curve of his jaw.

He groaned, then gently shoved her hand aside. "You'd better leave now," he said, clenching his teeth. "No—don't," he said when she took a step forward. "I'm warning you, Valerie. I can only take so much."

"But—"

"Just leave! And lock the damned door."

Her chest so tight she couldn't speak, she turned and strode to her room. She closed the door separating them, but didn't throw the bolt. If he came to her, she wouldn't stop him. She couldn't. She loved him too much.

She flung herself on the bed, trying to reason, trying to tell herself that loving him was the biggest mistake of her life.

*Think, Valerie!* she told herself. And she did. All night long. And what she decided during those long, dark hours was that she should take a chance. A man like Hale Donovan came along once in a lifetime, and she should trust him. Not tonight, but maybe tomorrow, and if things turned out as she'd hoped, for the rest of her life.

He'd asked her to marry him, hadn't he? Tomorrow she intended to find out if the offer still held.

She loved him, and that was that. Now she had the chance to be his bride.

Thoughts of love and marriage, of bearing Hale Donovan's children, flitted through her mind as she dozed fitfully. Yes, she loved him, and yes, she could trust him.

As the gray streaks of dawn filtered through her small window, she dozed, smiling to herself.

Yes, she'd accept Hale's marriage proposal. Yes, she'd throw off the chains of this charade. And yes, she'd make love to him. Everything would be perfect, she thought, finally drifting into a trouble-free sleep.

## Chapter Eleven

The next morning, while William and Beth were spending a few final hours in Victoria, the most beautiful, statuesque woman Valerie had ever set eyes on strolled onto *The Regina*. With flashing jade-green eyes, lustrous black hair, creamy white skin and pouty lips, she boarded as if she owned the yacht.

"Leigh!" Regina gasped, shooting Valerie a questioning glance.

*Leigh? As in Leigh Carmichael?*

"This *is* a surprise!" Regina gushed.

Leigh laughed throatily. "I thought you were expecting me." Before saying anything else, she leaned over the deck rail and called to the dock. "Could you bring the bags up?"

Stunned, Valerie watched as a cabbie, his car still idling on the dock, hauled several oversized bags onto the deck. Leigh paid him, then flopped onto a chaise and slipped her hat from her head. "Where is Hale?"

"Oh, he's on board somewhere," Regina replied, glancing anxiously at Valerie.

Leigh grinned. "Won't he be surprised? He wanted me to join him in San Francisco, but I couldn't get away. I was in Europe, you know." She sighed and, holding her straw hat by the crown, fanned herself. "Lord, it's warm!" Spying a pitcher of iced tea, she asked, "Do you mind?"

"Help yourself," Regina answered.

Valerie's stomach twisted. So Hale had asked Leigh to pose as his fiancée and she'd had the pride to decline. Now what? And why had he lied? He'd sworn his affair with Leigh was long over. If so, how did she know where to find him? Valerie twisted her hands in the folds of her skirt.

"Where is everybody?" Leigh poured herself a full glass of tea from the glass pitcher and held the glass to her forehead, emitting a contented sigh.

"Mom and Dad are in town. They'll be back soon. Stewart's with Hale, and Valerie and I were just up here talking."

Leigh swung her gaze to Valerie as if seeing her for the first time. "You're a friend of Regina's?"

Valerie felt perspiration dot her back, and it took all her willpower to keep her gaze steady with Leigh's. "We've become friends on the cruise," she said, hoping to sound noncommittal... when her world was actually falling apart. Obviously Hale's relationship with Leigh was far from over.

Regina, looking uncomfortable, made hasty, vague introductions. Where once Regina might have been amused at the awkward situation, now she actually seemed unnerved. "This is Valerie Pryce. Leigh Carmichael."

Valerie forced a smile onto her frozen face. "I've heard a lot about you," she offered lamely.

Leigh drew her perfect dark brows together. "You must know Stewart." She glanced at the ring on Valerie's left hand and began to smile. Her green eyes twinkled merrily. "Don't tell me—you're going to marry him!" Leigh cried, throwing her head back and laughing. "I can't believe it. Someone's actually tying down the elusive Stewart Stowell!"

Collecting herself, Valerie shook her head. "No, actually, I've only known him a short while."

"But the ring—I thought . . ." Leigh stopped herself. Her beautiful face washed of color.

There was no reason to lie. Valerie was backed into a corner. "I'm here with Hale," she admitted as calmly as possible.

To her credit, Leigh composed herself and sipped her tea. "Hale?"

"Yes."

Studying the ice cubes in her glass, she said, "So that's how you've heard of me." Sighing, she asked, "Did Hale bother to mention we're engaged?"

Valerie felt as if she'd been kicked in the stomach.

"No, I don't suppose he did," Leigh decided with a dismissive wave of her hand.

Regina glanced at Valerie. "But that's impossible—"

"Just because we haven't been together for a few weeks?" Leigh asked coyly, though she seemed more nervous than when she'd first boarded. "Okay, I'll admit that when Hale called and invited me to join him, I was a little uncomfortable. We hadn't announced our engagement, not officially, but what better place than this?" She gestured to the teak deck, rigging, flapping sails and sun-dappled water.

"Yes, what better place?" Valerie whispered, her throat burning. All those lies. Last night. All those vows of love. How often had he said them? To how many women? In her heart she wanted to believe that she was the only one—that he wouldn't lie to her, but he had.

Regina frowned. "I don't understand. Valerie and Hale—"

"Work together," Valerie cut in, shooting Regina a look that could kill. The less said here, the better. She didn't know what Leigh's game was, but Valerie thought she'd better hear her out before she made any rash statements about being engaged to Hale herself. After all, her engagement was a phony. Maybe Leigh was lying, but maybe not.

"I'm a little embarrassed to admit this," Leigh went on as she poured herself another glass of tea. "But Hale called while I was in Marseilles, and we had this stupid little argument. I even told him I didn't want to show up and announce that we were engaged when it hadn't been in any of the papers." She caught the eye of one of the crew members. "Oh, Jim, would you see to my bags, please?" she asked, pointing to the mountain of matching luggage near the main sail.

"Leigh?" Hale's voice cut through the warm morning air.

Valerie froze, but saw him from the corner of her eye.

His expression murderous, his hands planted firmly on his hips, he stood near the stairs. He flicked his gaze to Leigh before focusing squarely on Valerie.

Leigh's features relaxed, and her eyes sparkled. "Oh, there you are!" she cried, crossing the deck quickly and wrapping her arms around his neck. "I thought for a minute I'd gotten on the wrong boat!"

*No, that's my mistake,* Valerie thought anxiously.

"You've met Valerie," he said.

"Just!"

Hale didn't move. His face was carved in granite. "What are you doing here?" he asked, peeling her arms away from him.

"Oh, please," she cooed, "don't tell me you're still angry! I'm sorry I didn't meet you in San Francisco, but it was just so inconvenient. And you surprised me."

"*I* surprised *you*?" he asked, glancing at Valerie. Dear God, what was Leigh doing here? Had she heard about his engagement? And Valerie—he watched her lower herself weakly down in one of the deck chairs.

Leigh fingered his collar. "Most people aren't proposed to long distance—"

"I don't remember proposing to you," he said calmly.

Leigh waved her hand against his argument. "Oh, come on! You called me in Marseilles and asked me to marry you. This trip was supposed to be a celebration of our engagement."

"I think you misunderstood," he said through tight lips as he peeled her fingers from his shirt.

"But—"

Moving away from Leigh, Hale dropped a proprietary hand on Valerie's shoulder. The minute his skin touched hers, he felt her shaking. "You said you already met Valerie."

Leigh nodded.

"Good. Because *she's* the woman I intend to marry."

"Marry? *Her?*" Leigh moved her lips in protest. "Pardon me?"

"It's all right," Valerie said, standing quickly despite the clench of Hale's fingers over her shoulder. There wasn't any reason to drag this out. Regina already knew something was very wrong, and Beth and William Stowell, chatting together, arms linked, were boarding.

Hale's deception was over.

William looked up, caught site of Leigh and ground to a stop. Beth, too, saw the unlikely group. "Oh, my," she whispered.

A frown as deep as the Grand Canyon crossed William Stowell's round face. "Well, Leigh," he finally said when the silence stretched long. "I didn't expect to see you here."

"Obviously," she said dryly, shooting Hale a pouty glance.

Valerie's stomach flip-flopped, and she wished there were some way of escaping, but Hale clamped his hand more firmly over her shoulder. "There's been a mix-up, that's all," he said. "I did call Leigh in Marseilles," he said slowly, narrowing his eyes on the gorgeous woman, "and we did discuss marriage and this trip."

Valerie sagged a little.

"But she wasn't interested in cutting short her vacation. In the meantime I met Valerie. She came into the office on an interview and I knew then that she was the woman I wanted to spend the rest of my life with."

"Her?" Leigh cried, disbelieving.

"Leigh, I'd like you to meet my fiancée," Hale said as Valerie slowly rose.

Valerie just wanted to escape, but Hale dropped his arm to her waist and held her firmly against him with strong fingers. Unless she wanted to cause more of a scene, she didn't dare move.

"I think there's been a mistake," Valerie said.

"A big one," Leigh agreed vehemently. "I just flew halfway around the world!" She turned her sparking green eyes on Hale and wagged a furious finger in his face. "You! You asked me to meet you—sent me the itinerary! How could you find someone else to pretend to fall in love with you in so short a time?"

"This isn't an act," Hale insisted.

"Oh, come on, Hale. Get real!" Leigh gestured to the Stowells. "How dumb do you think they are?"

Valerie gasped.

"That's enough," Beth insisted.

But Leigh couldn't stop. "You don't expect them to believe that you, a confirmed bachelor, are going to marry a woman you barely know!" She glanced at the rest of the group, as if hoping to confirm what was so obviously apparent to her.

"I think this has gone on long enough," Valerie said. "Hale can explain. Now if you'll excuse me a minute—"

"You're not going anywhere," Hale said.

"Watch me."

"Valerie, please—"

But she couldn't stand to hear another lie. "We'll talk later," she said, tears burning the back of her eyes. Now she was the one who was lying. She had no intention, if she ever got off this damned boat, of seeing him again. "If you'll excuse me," she said to the group in general as she shrugged off Hale's arm and headed to the stairs.

"I love you," he shouted, and all other sounds seemed to disappear.

Valerie stumbled. If only she could believe him! She glanced back, saw the crowd and realized he was still playing his role. Swallowing the thick, hot lump in her throat, she groped for the rail to the stairs. She wouldn't break down. Not now. But her eyes burned. Fighting blinding tears, she ran to her room.

Why had she ever agreed to this crazy scheme? In the past few days she'd begun to care for the Stowells, and now they'd know her only as a phony and a fake, a woman who had intentionally deceived them, made them look like fools!

Feeling about one inch tall, she threw open the doors of her closet and hauled out her two small bags. There had to be some way she could talk to Beth and explain. Or could she? And what about Hale? Dear God, how would she ever forget him?

Fingers shaking, she snapped open the bags and began tossing her clothes, not the elegant dresses he'd bought for her, but her very own clothes, into suitcases.

"You don't have to leave." Hale's voice, though barely a whisper, echoed loudly through the room.

Turning, she found him filling the doorway, just as he'd filled her life for the past two weeks. "Of course I do," she returned shakily, hating the fact that he would see her so close to tears.

"If you'd just listen to me—"

"No, Hale, this time you listen to me," she said, her eyes burning, her chin quaking as she thrust it forward. "The game is over. Over! I don't know what you're going to tell William Stowell, or if it matters anymore. Leigh's here, so she can keep Regina at bay. Now all you have to do is convince William you made a mistake with your women—but that you're still interested in his company."

"It's not that simple."

"It's as simple as you make it!"

She reached for the smaller bag, but he shut the door behind him and locked it. Her knees sagged, but she forced herself to remain upright.

"Hear me out, Valerie," he insisted, his back to the door. His face looked drawn, and his hands actually trembled when he lifted them to shove his hair from his face. "Just stay long enough to let me convince you I love you."

"We're alone, Hale. You don't have to pretend."

"I'm not pretending, damn it! I love you, Valerie. You have to believe me."

His cocky smile had disappeared, and even his anger seemed to have faded. His face was lined and his eyes sincere.

Oh, dear God, she wanted to trust him. But all she had to do was think about Leigh Carmichael, think about the lies, the deception of William Stowell, her part in the scheme, and realize what a consummate actor Hale Donovan was. Hadn't he proved his chameleonlike ability to change roles time and time again in the past few weeks?

Her throat was so dry she could barely speak. When she did, her voice was the barest of whispers. "Please... Leave. Before we say or do something we'll regret."

"Too late for that," he said. "I regret not being honest with you from the first. The reason I chose you, Valerie, was that from the first time I set eyes on you I knew you were a woman I could love."

"No..." she choked out. *Don't believe him! He's lied all his life to get what he wanted! No one knows that better than you!*

"I want you to marry me," he said slowly, his voice even, his eyes flinty. He didn't move one step closer, just stood at the door, quietly insisting.

Valerie felt herself breaking inside. "I have to leave, Hale."

"Not until you say you'll marry me."

"And then what, Hale?" she snapped. "We'll go back to San Francisco and then what?"

"We'll get married."

"You're not serious!"

"More serious than I've been about anything in my life," he said solemnly.

He seemed sincere, but, then he was a natural actor, a man with a purpose, a man who had bought and sold her just to buy another man's company. "Goodbye, Hale," she said, holding her bags, waiting for him to move, praying she'd find the strength to escape.

He took one step closer. "Trust me, Valerie."

"Hale?" Leigh's voice floated down the short hall, followed by her quick footsteps.

Valerie grabbed the door handle. "She's looking for you."

"She means nothing to me."

Valerie tightened her fingers on the door handle. "Well, someone had better tell her."

"I will."

She yanked open the door, only to have him slam it shut with his shoulder. "Please, Valerie."

She blinked hard. "I want to believe you, Hale, but I can't. You told me from the beginning that this was only a temporary position, an act, all part of our agreement. You can't expect me to believe that now, after everything you've said and done, that you're in love with me."

His smile was sad. "I do love you. And I think you're in love with me, as well. You're just too stubborn to admit it."

"Stubborn?" she repeated.

"As a mule."

"Hale?" Leigh's voice was impatient. "Will someone kindly tell me what's going on?"

"That's your cue," Valerie said as Leigh pounded on Hale's stateroom door.

"Wait for me," he said as he slipped into the hallway.

Valerie didn't move. Not until she was sure Hale had sequestered Leigh. Then, before she did anything as stupid as listen to her foolish heart, she pulled the diamond ring from her finger, set it in a dish near her bed and silently crept down the hall. With any luck she'd be able to say hasty goodbyes to the Stowells, grab a cab and take the first flight out of Victoria.

# Chapter Twelve

I just don't understand," Valerie's mother said after Valerie's lengthy explanation. "It was all an *act*?"

Standing at the door of her mother's apartment, Valerie shifted from one foot to the other. "That's right. Hale and I never intended to get married."

"So you lied. To me."

"Yes, Mom, I lied," Valerie admitted, feeling like a schoolgirl again.

"Too bad." Anna sighed. "You know, I kind of liked him."

"Donovan? You about went through the roof when I told you we were planning to get married."

Anna grinned. "It was a shock, I'll grant you that. But you know I want nothing more than for you to get married and be happy."

"With Hale Donovan?" Valerie shook her head. "The man's impossible."

"Besides," Anna said wistfully, "it's time I had some grandchildren to spoil."

"Mom!" Valerie gasped. "What are you saying? You're still not recovered—"

"But I'm getting there." Anna laughed. "And grandkids might just be the medicine I need."

Valerie rolled her eyes. "Save me," she whispered.

"Well, maybe things will change," Anna decided. "You *are* working for Donovan Enterprises, right?" She handed Shamus, stuffed unhappily in his cat carrier, to her daughter.

"Not anymore."

"But you had a contract."

"I think I blew it," Valerie said with a sigh. She'd only been back in San Francisco four hours and it seemed like an eternity since she'd left Hale.

Shamus meowed loudly.

"I know, I know," Valerie said to the cat. "Look, Mom, I'll call you tomorrow. I just wanted you to know the truth before it hit the papers."

"And when will that be?"

"I have no idea," Valerie admitted as she closed the door behind her.

Outside, she climbed back into her car and headed home. The day had passed in a whirlwind of planes and cabs. She'd stopped by her apartment only long enough to jump in her car, drive straight to her mother's apartment and collect Shamus.

"And now what do we do?" she asked the tabby as dusk settled over the city, draping the hills in a cloak of purple light. "Back to square one?"

Shamus didn't deign to answer.

Valerie parked in her usual spot. Balancing the cat carrier and two suitcases, she trudged up the three flights to her apartment, jabbed her key into the lock and kicked open the door.

"About time you showed up," Hale drawled.

Valerie stopped dead in her tracks. Shamus hissed. She dropped one suitcase, and Hale, blast the man, had the audacity to smile. Draped insolently on her couch, the heels of his Nikes propped on a chair, he flashed her that heart-stopping grin she found so irresistible. His jaw was dark with the shadow of a beard, his mouth framed by deep lines, his eyes as warm and erotic as ever. Dressed in worn jeans and a beat-up leather jacket, he looked as if he belonged here.

Just the sight of him nearly broke her heart. Why couldn't she force herself to hate him?

"Close the door, Val."

"Wh-what are you doing here?"

"I think we have some unfinished business."

"But . . . how?" She glanced around the room. "How did you get in?"

"You left an extra set of keys in that." He pointed to a beach bag she'd obviously forgotten while escaping *The Regina.*

She leaned against the wall. "And you couldn't resist breaking and entering."

"I didn't break—just entered."

Though her heart was galloping a thousand miles a minute, Valerie tried to keep some rein on her thoughts. She shrugged out of her coat and let Shamus free. The cat made a beeline to the French doors. "What about the Stowells?"

Hale cocked one dark brow. "What about them?"

"Where are they?"

"Still yachting up north, I guess."

"You don't know?"

"Nope." Stretching, he climbed off her couch, walked forward and closed the door she'd left open. "And I don't care."

"Give me a break—"

"You've had your break," he said evenly, though his smile faded a little. Standing so close she could see his pupils dilate, he said softly, "I told William Stowell I wasn't interested in his company." He fingered a wayward strand of her hair, and his touch sent tingles sliding down her spine. "Stewart's ecstatic about the turn of events. William's mad, and Beth—she told me I'd better chase after you."

"So that's why you're here?"

"Nope."

His breath fanned her face and his fingers were playing havoc with her senses. Valerie swallowed. "Then why?"

"Guess."

"I couldn't."

"Because of you."

Her heart leaped. Her fingers clenched. *Don't believe him, Valerie. He wants something!* "Me? But why?"

"Because this afternoon you walked out on ten thousand dollars and the best job you'll ever find in this city. If you read the contract you signed with me carefully, you'll realize you signed a noncompete agreement."

She winced a little, remembering the contract. "You'd hold me to it?"

"Of course I would."

She narrowed her eyes. "But why?"

"Because you're supposed to work for me for the next six months. Your idea, remember?"

"But not as your fiancée."

"No. As my assistant. And my wife."

The words stunned her. "Your wife?"

"Marry me, Val."

Was he serious? Her palms began to sweat. "I don't think we can convince William Stowell we're still engaged."

"This has nothing to do with Stowell."

"No? Then what?"

"You and me," he drawled.

It was all she could do to stand her ground. Her heart hammered, and she licked her lips nervously. "Don't you think this has gone on long enough?"

"A lifetime isn't enough."

Valerie stared at him. She wanted to believe him—dear God, if only she could! But just this morning another woman had showed up as her replacement—a woman who had known all about the cruise, a woman ready to pose as Hale's fiancée.

"Look, I don't know why you're here, or who you're trying to convince you have all the right intentions, but it doesn't matter. And if you really intend to uphold the noncompete clause, I'll find another job. In another field."

Hale shook his head. "You wanted to work for me, didn't you? You wanted to prove you could be my assistant?"

"Yes."

"And now I'm giving you the chance to be my wife."

Slowly he reached into his jacket pocket and withdrew his handkerchief. "You forgot something besides your bag on the yacht." Opening the cloth, he held out the diamond ring he'd bought her less than two weeks before.

She shook her head, fighting the crazy urge to throw her arms around him and tell him that she'd love to marry him, that she'd willingly spend the rest of her life with him, that in her wildest fantasies she dreamed of only him.

Instead she kept her voice reasonably calm. "We don't even know each other."

"I know all I have to."

Her head was spinning, her throat constricting. Things were moving too fast. Though she knew she should yank her hand back as he placed the ring on her finger, she didn't.

"Come on." Taking her hand in his, he unlocked the French doors and stepped onto her deck.

Shamus darted behind the planter. The sounds of the city seemed far in the distance, the lights winking on the bay reflections of the stars.

"So," Hale said as a breeze teased his hair, "what do you want to know about me?"

"How about your family for starters?"

He grimaced, his eyes becoming as dark as the night. Seconds stretched to minutes. "All right," he finally said. "I never knew my father. He left before I was born."

"And your mother?" she asked, seeing a pain in his eyes.

"My mother." His expression hardened. "My mother gave me up when I was two. I don't remember her."

"When you were two?" she whispered, her heart nearly stopping.

"I was in the way. You see, she found herself a wealthy man, a man who wasn't interested in raising someone else's kid."

"Oh, Hale, no..." Valerie whispered, the tears she'd battled all day filling her eyes. "But your grandparents...?"

"Were dead. I grew up in foster homes. Some were okay. Others..." He shrugged, frowning and stuffing his hands into his pockets. "Well, it all worked out, I guess.

I've never seen my mother since the day she left me." His voice was emotionless, but Valerie had to struggle against her own tears. She ached for the little unloved boy he'd once been. No wonder he thought money was so important—that he could buy whatever he wanted. His mother had abandoned him in pursuit of the almighty dollar.

"I'm sorry."

"It wasn't your fault." He offered her a weary smile. "Anything else you want to know about me?"

"Everything," she admitted.

"Everything." He let out a long breath. "That might take a while."

"I've got the time," she whispered, trusting him at last.

Moonlight caught in his eyes. "Do you?"

"If forever's long enough."

He blinked, as if astounded. Then a smile spread slowly from one side of his face to the other. "Why, Ms. Pryce, are you proposing to me?"

Valerie laughed. "Or propositioning you. Whatever you want."

"Oh, no. This time we tie the knot. Before you have a chance to escape." With that he wrapped strong arms around her and held her tight. His lips hovered over hers.

Her pulse thundered, and a warmth, liquid and soft, stirred deep inside. She wound her arms around his neck and held him close. There was so much to learn about him—so much to love. And she had the rest of her life.

When he finally lifted his head, he rested his chin on her crown. "I love you, you know."

"And I love you."

"Lake Tahoe is only a few hours away," he said, glancing at his watch. "We could be married by midnight."

"Tonight?" she gasped.

"Tonight."

"But what about Shamus?"

"We'll be back tomorrow."

"And my mother—"

"Can read about it in the newspapers."

Valerie laughed, thinking of her mother's response. "You know, she just might like that."

"I love you, Valerie Pryce."

"And I love you." She gazed up at him and couldn't help smiling. "But this won't get you out of that contract. I still intend to work for Donovan Enterprises and prove that I can handle the job as your personal assistant."

Hale laughed. "You already have."

"Don't think you can weasel out of it."

"Wouldn't dream of it," he countered. "In fact, I think we should draw up a new agreement. One that states exactly what your duties will be as my wife, what will be expected of you, how you'll spend your days."

"Not on your life, Donovan. This time the only piece of paper we need is the marriage license."

"Amen," he whispered, kissing her again, drawing her into the circle of his arms and holding her as if he never would let her go. "Stay with me forever."

"I will," she vowed, and she meant it.

\*     \*     \*     \*     \*

# *Silhouette* ❦ *Romance*®

# COMING NEXT MONTH

**#718 SECOND TIME LUCKY—Victoria Glenn**
*A Diamond Jubilee Book!*
Ailing Aunt Lizbeth glowed with health after Miles Crane kissed
her man-shy goddaughter Lara MacEuan. If Miles had his way,
his frail aunt would be on a rapid road to recovery!

**#719 THE NESTING INSTINCT—Elizabeth August**
Zeke Wilson's cynical view of love had him propose a marriage of
convenience to Meg Delany. Could his in-name-only bride
conceal her longing for a marriage of love?

**#720 MOUNTAIN LAUREL—Donna Clayton**
Laurel Morgan went to the mountains for rest and
relaxation... but Ranger Michael Walker knew fair game when
he saw it! The hunt was on, but who was chasing whom?

**#721 SASSAFRAS STREET—Susan Kalmes**
Callie Baker was furious when the man who outbid her at an
antique auction turned out to be Nick Logan, her new boss. Nick,
on the other hand, was thrilled....

**#722 IN THE FAMILY WAY—Melodie Adams**
Fiercely independent divorcée Sarah Jordan was quite in the
family way—and had no plans for marriage. But smitten Steven
Carlisle had plans of his own—to change her mind!

**#723 THAT SOUTHERN TOUCH—Stella Bagwell**
Workaholic Whitney Drake ran from her fast-paced New York
life to the Louisiana bayou—and right into the arms of Caleb
Jones. But could his loving touch convince her to stay forever?

# AVAILABLE THIS MONTH:

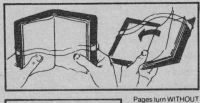
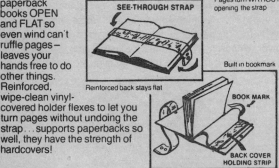

## DIAMOND JUBILEE
## CELEBRATION!

It's Silhouette Books' tenth anniversary, and what better way to celebrate than to toast *you*, our readers, for making it all possible. Each month in 1990, we'll present you with a DIAMOND JUBILEE Silhouette Romance written by an all-time favorite author!

Welcome the new year with *Ethan*—a LONG, TALL TEXANS book by Diana Palmer. February brings Brittany Young's *The Ambassador's Daughter*. Look for *Never on Sundae* by Rita Rainville in March, and in April you'll find *Harvey's Missing* by Peggy Webb. Victoria Glenn, Lucy Gordon, Annette Broadrick, Dixie Browning and many more have special gifts of love waiting for you with their DIAMOND JUBILEE Romances.

Be sure to look for the distinctive DIAMOND JUBILEE emblem, and share in Silhouette's celebration. Saying thanks has never been so romantic. . . .

SRJUB-1